TO SANDY AND KELLY ROBERTS

Sheila Roberts

Coming in and other stories

JUSTIFIED PRESS

Justified Press
A division of
Ashanti Publishing (Pty) Ltd
P.O. Box 5091
Rivonia
Johannesburg 2128

First published 1993

ISBN 0 947451 22 6

Typeset by PhotoPrints

Printed and bound by ABC Book Printers

Contents

Contents

COMING IN

Luc, with Maman on his arm, entered the Hotel Woltemade which was, it seemed, all they could afford in this new country. Papa came behind, treading in their shadows and carrying the overnight bags. Luc felt tired; his body had loosened uncomfortably, and he no longer cared, as he had when they left the ship, that Maman's make-up was over-emphatic and inexact, especially round the mouth, and that Papa's head had developed a tendency to wobble on its vein-patterned and bristly neck. He really was too tired.

Luc was over-mature for seventeen, sombrely adult, and limply thin: untaut, delicate. So he tired easily. He might not have felt so attenuated had they not been forced to stand so long in the hammering sun at the teeming docks, waiting for a taxi and taunted by a wind that seemed to blow directly from over a desert.

A young Coloured man with a serious rosebud mouth and large unavoidable spectacles attended to them at the reception desk, and Luc booked a room containing three beds. Another Coloured youth, wearing a shabbier uniform than the first (he had probably just started his portering job and had to use his predecessor's cast-offs, Luc surmised) led them upstairs to their room. Luc allowed Maman and Papa to go before him up the stairs. Maman's short muscular legs lifted laboriously, her feet trying to cling to wide shoes with warped heels that clunked on the uncarpeted stairs. Papa climbed like some splay-footed bird, his body bent, his neck thrust forward. Luc's gut churned with pity and annoyance.

The room they were given overlooked a busy street.

There was a scratched wardrobe in it and a washbasin.

1

Also, a small bedside cupboard containing two very new bibles and an old enamel chamber pot.

'Don't touch that!' hissed Luc as Maman reached out her hand to investigate. Luc opened the wardrobe and stared morosely at the twisted wire coathangers suspended like ill fortune from the copper rail. The wardrobe smelled of camphor or eucalyptus and old newspapers (or was it socks?). Maman had turned the faucet on over the basin, but only a subterranean gurgling issued forth. No water. Three uneven beds stretched thick with disgusting secrets under the thin afternoon light. Luc braced himself to toss, irreverently, the overnight bags onto one of them. He had taken them impatiently from Papa's moist grasp, irritated by his father's hoarse breathing.

Later, when they had unpacked a few necessary clothes and toiletries, and had closed the door on the porter who had got the water turned on, they changed, washed their faces and brushed their hair. Then they sat on their beds to plan the next move. Now they became aware of voices growing louder, mingling in animated conversation, and echoing through the floorboards and threadbare mats. They listened, appalled.

'The bar!' said Maman. 'We are situ*ate* on top of the bar!'

'*Merde!*' said Luc.

They continued sitting in silence. Luc knew Maman was praying.

At seven they ventured timidly downstairs, walking almost on tiptoe. The voices from the bar, clearer now, spoke and shouted in an unfamiliar language and the laughter seemed threatening, cruel. They hesitated, dreading to offend. They looked into the dining-room. It was small, empty of diners, and had a lingering smell of vinegar and old mutton fat. The linen was shabby from many old stains and slapdash washings, and the two black waiters talking together in the far corner glanced indifferently at them and went on with their conversation. As they stood, grouped in the doorway, looking at the uninviting tables, they heard a woman's voice say: 'Ag, must you block a person's path, hey?'

Luc leapt aside and Maman and Papa shuffled.

'Thanks hey.'

A woman in a bright head-scarf, with outlined eyes and lipstick that looked like jam, pushed past them. She wore a faded red taffeta shift dress and had hooked her painted toes into thong-sandals that flip-smacked across the linoleum.

'Hey, let's have some bloody service here!' she called to the waiters as she dropped into a chair. Luc stared at the overflow of hips.

'Putain,' murmured Maman.

'Shsh ...' whispered Luc.

'We come back in a moment, *non*?' suggested Maman.

'Yes,' said Luc.

They walked up and down the street, Maman on Luc's arm and Papa behind, and they looked curiously into the shops. There seemed to be a predominance of second-hand clothing stores, pawnbrokers and radio repair-shops on that street. They paused silently in front of a window presenting sheet music, tarnished wind instruments, large gaudy guitars and old turntables. They passed a dark, silent dairy and a dry-cleaners, and then came to a fish-and-chips shop. They stopped and smelled the hot odours of frying fish and chopped potatoes.

'I have honger,' said Papa, trying his English.

'I am hungry, *hungry*,' corrected Luc.

'Yes, yes, I *yam*,' said Papa.

'Darling, we cannot eat tonight in that hotel,' said Maman. 'Loose women ... you never know ... some infection.'

'Maman, don't be stupid,' said Luc but without conviction.

'Well, we wait and see ...' said Maman, stalling.

'We wait and see for *what*, Maman?'

'We check and knives and forks and the glasses. Where there are whores ...'

'Maman, there are whores everywhere. In Blida, in Paris, in Cape Town.'

'In Youhaneesboorg?' suggested Papa.

Luc and Maman clung to each other as they laughed. 'Johannesburg, Papa; *Johannesburg*!'

Papa merely shook his head in mock-sadness.

'Anyway,' said Luc, sobering, 'listen to me. If you use the toilet ... are you listening Papa? If you use it, make sure you first cover the seat with sheets and sheets of paper.'

Maman nodded.

'We must all be very careful.'

'Yes, darling,' said Maman.

They entered the fish-and-chips shop and pointed to the hot chips and the oily red sausages, deciding they would be safer for the stomach than fish. Luc bought a pint of milk, and they carried it all back to their hotel. Feeling guilty, almost criminal, they climbed the stairs close to the far wall, holding the hot, newspaper-wrapped parcels half-hidden.

That night Luc lay awake in his bed, looking up at the shapes of light and dark on the ceiling in their dim room. The lights from the street and the passing traffic kept the room from being dark, and the voices from the bar maintained a steady hum which rose and fell with its own rhythm until after one in the morning.

It had been foolish thinking that emigrating to a new country would be like entering the Promised Land, he now realized. But still, he had expected and partly still did ... something. Something to delight the heart. Some symbol of welcome, some presage. Perhaps in Johannesburg, the golden ... Although Luc's eyes felt heavy and were, he expected, blue-smudged, they could not rest under their dry lids. He watched, caught in circular thoughts. The murky ceiling hanging over him held vermin perhaps, and the sighing mattresses too. He lay stiff, unmoving and miserable, his flesh itching. If he once began turning he would not be able to stop but would writhe and toss himself into a frenzy and wake his parents. Better to remain still.

What had they expected, after all? Their money, their property was gone, gone, confiscated by the *Front de Libération Nationale*. Only the jewels that Maman had hidden remained. Why should the people here offer them fine hospitality? Why should they? Yet this Hotel Woltemade was a hotel for white people, and white people, he had been told, were all wealthy in South Africa, and opportunity was limitless. He hesitated to whisper the word *barbares* even to himself, but for the moment he was, well, bitter. For instance, where were the showers? Down the corridor there was a bathroom with a chipped bathtub, yellowed round the plug-hole and offering a porous criss-crossed plank *thing* for a bathmat. Did one have to lie in one's own filth, and the filth of twenty other residents? Even the confounded Arabs knew better than that. Unexpectedly, he remembered the little silver dishes Maman used for the gemlike orblets of preserve they would taste with their chilled almond-water at sundown as they sat on the patio under the vines. And the brass dish for the Turkish coffee. On the mild autumn evenings the poplar leaves would lie motionless, in subdued passion, against the sky mottling from pale green to orange. Papa would bring out the backgammon and sit waiting for Oncle Henri to come over. He, Luc, has not been strong and could not work on the estate, but he could add figures for Maman and had learnt to keep books. Before the trouble.

Papa turned onto his back and his tongue sucked against his palate. Maman was snoring softly, her hands clasped across her large stomach still woven into the beads she had been telling.

When you were old you slept easily; perhaps because the worst had already happened, thought Luc.

They stood rocking against each other in the corridor of the moving train, waiting for the railway employee to finish making up their beds. An unending, uninhabited landscape of stubbly plains and angular hillocks flowed along beyond the window. Papa shivered although it was not cold.

'*Qu'est-ce qu'il y'a?*' asked Maman.

'That man, he not feeshid?' he begged.

Maman chortled throatily, her sound delighting Luc. He clutched her plump forearm.

'You stupid,' gargled Maman. 'You big stupid! It is finished not feeshid.'

'So, this is not my language,' said Papa, but he also smiled.

'Remember not to say pick*less* for pickles,' reminded Luc, hoping to make Maman laugh again. But the railwayman interrupted.

'Awright, lady and gentlemens, your beds are made.'

Luc, immediately hopeful, jingled change in his pocket and tipped the man two shillings.

'You are also stupid,' hissed Maman. 'I have two stupid men with me.'

'Nevermind, Maman. Nevermind,' said Luc airily.

They stood in the compartment surveying the three folded blue-blanketed beds.

'Do you believe that *these* are clean, Maman?' Luc asked.

'Oui, oui, these are fumi*gate*, these are fumi*gate*,' insisted Papa.

'How can you know?' laughed Maman.

'I know, I know,' said Papa seriously.

'Ah … well …' said Luc. He looked into the washbasin and pulled and pushed the stopper.

'I think I'll go and look where the toilets are and where the dining-room is,' he said. 'You two wait here. All right?' Adult and capable, Luc straightened his jacket and re-entered the corridor. Some way down he stopped and thought of returning to their compartment. He wanted to remind Maman that she should not urinate in the basin. He knew she hated using public toilets, and he had to stop her from so using the basin in their cabin on the ship. Deciding that he wouldn't want to embarrass her, he pressed on. But he felt worried.

Late the next day the train stood tediously long at a country platform across which a throng of Africans, mostly wearing coloured blankets and wide straw hats, moved noisily. They carried boxes and cardboard suitcases on their shoulders. Some were whistling high, monotonously and continuously; others chanted, shuffled dance-steps and laughed. Maman and Papa sat close together, horrified, while Luc rested his head back in pretended indifference.

'*Les sauvages ...*' whispered Papa.

'Darling, I think we make a big mistake,' said Maman softly. 'We should go with Oncle Henry to Osstraalia.'

Luc turned his head and focused on two black men who wore their khaki trousers tied under their knees with rope and who were dancing flirtatiously, with high steps, at a group of women sitting fatly amid their bundles on the platform gravel. They sat as if they planned to stay some time, and the men made eyes and universally recognizable gestures.

'No, no, Maman. No. This country is better for us. People say there are more jobs and more money. And there are servants. Do you want to polish and scrub floors at your age? And do washing and ironing? So ... wait ... don't be prejudiced.'

'*Tous ces noirs,*' murmured Papa.

'I shall have to pray to God,' declared Maman, perforce resigned.

From Germiston Station onward the train crawled slowly, steadily, across widths of line, parallel and interweaving, and through what looked like a densely-built industrial area. Now the corridors were packed with the passengers, the younger ones hanging out of the windows to spot Johannesburg first. Luc stood too, but could not bring himself to hang. But his heart seemed to be blocking his breathing and he had clamped his lips, tight and manly. Just behind him, in the open compartment, Maman and Papa sat closer together than they had ever seemed to want to sit in their married life. They waited for their son to tell them they were there. That things were all right.

Then they were under shelters and a glassed-in dome and fluorescent lights spelling JOHANNESBURG, and young show-off men had doors open, ready to leap and run and laugh. And Luc's brief harsh surge of joy sent the saliva into his mouth. The golden …

A white porter who seemed determined not to utter a word, helped them with their baggage and trundled it along swiftly, making them trot pantingly after him. He took them to the taxi rank and Luc, uncertain, gave him a five-shilling piece. But this time Maman said nothing.

'We want a hotel …' Luc said to the taxi driver.

'What hotel?'

'One for about … ah … two pounds a night,' stuttered Luc, not sure. 'Do you know of …?'

'All right, get in.'

They drove dangerously up a wide city street closed in with tall buildings and handsome shops, and festooned with overhead bus wires. Luc and Papa watched the traffic and the well-dressed people feverishly, but Maman closed her eyes and felt for the rosary beads in her purse. Eventually, to

Luc's disappointment, they turned down narrower streets where the shops were mostly car lots and auto repairs. Then they were in a dingier street of small apartment buildings and private hotels with, at each street corner, the wooden swing-doors of a bar. Luc wondered if he could bear another experience of demeanment. Maybe if they paid more …

'This place'll charge you about two quid a day, I think,' said the driver, stopping. It was too late for Luc to change his mind.

At the reception desk a large middle-aged woman surveyed them through slanting ornamental spectacles.

'Yes … I think I can let you have one double room with bath and a single room.'

'How much?' asked Luc.

'Two pounds five shillings each. That's with breakfast.'

Luc looked at Maman who shrugged.

'Yes. We'll take these rooms.'

The woman swung the register round toward Luc. 'Fill this in, will you.' She watched them with serious curiosity.

'You people foreigners?'

'We are from Algerie,' said Maman.

'From where?'

'Algeria,' said Luc. 'We are French.'

'Algeria, hey? But there's Arabs in Algeria, isn't there?'

'Of course. But we are French.'

'French, hey?'

'Yes.'

The woman turned to a numbered board bearing hooks from which some keys hung. She took down two keys attached to small pink planks and handed them to Luc.

'You are French, hey? You sure?'

'Yes, indeed we are French,' said Luc feeling the blood leave his face. He stared at the woman, opening his eyes widely and intently. She looked away uncomfortably.

'I've just got to make sure you're white,' she said. 'All right, then. Hey, Lazarus, come here man. Take these people to number twelve and fourteen.'

A black with a shaved head took all their luggage and led the way. This time Luc forgot to tip. He stood in the double room with his parents and registered the unremitting roar of traffic. Then he started crying noisily, gasping and choking in his own tears.

'*Mon Dieu,*' said Maman.

'Luc, Luc, what is it?' said Papa.

'Sit down, darling, sit. Maman will go and ask that woman for Aspro. You have done too much. Now you must rest. Maman will see to everything. Even you can lie down.'

'Rest, Luc, rest,' begged Papa.

But Luc would not lie down. He stood crying himself out and his parents stood watching, frightened and helpless and not daring to sit down themselves. Then he grew calmer, and blew his nose. 'It's okay ...' he hiccuped. 'But I do need some aspirin. I'll just wash my face and go down to the reception desk and ask for some.'

'Darling, Maman will go ...'

'No, no. I'm all right now.'

As Luc noiselessly, feeling wraithlike, approached the woman at the reception, he heard her talking on the telephone. 'Elsie, what I want to know is are Algerians white people? I mean *French* from Algeria? They look white, but just dark, like Eye-talians. You think they are? Awright then. Anyway, it's not my business, I suppose. I jus' don' want to catch flack from that Cohen. He's never here to see what's going on in his bloody hotel, but jus' let me make a mistake. You think it's awright? Awright Elsie, bye-bye.'

The woman turned and stared.

'Have you any aspirin to sell me?' asked Luc tightly.

'Aspirin?'

'Yes.' He controlled a sob pushing forward to his throat.

'You not feeling too hot?'

'Pardon me?'

'You got a headache?'

'Yes.'

'Well, I haven't got any to sell you, but I'll give you two from my purse.'

'Ah, no, no …'

'Ag yes, you can have them. Here.'

Luc allowed the woman to pour the aspirin into his palm.

'Thank you,' he said.

'Ag, that's awright.' Then softening, the woman said, 'I hope you like it here … in this country.'

'Yes, thank you … thank you.'

'It's a great country you know; finest in the world.'

'Indeed? Yes, yes …'

'Anyway, take those and lie down, see.'

'Yes, thank you again.'

As Luc climbed the stairs he looked down at the old, slightly porous aspirin tablets in his hand. He dropped them onto the soil of an aspidistra plant on the landing.

Luc reached the small insurance-agent's office at 8.20 a.m., but the door was still locked. He stood nervously, well out of the way of people hurrying to work, and hoping that he did not look too young or too inexperienced. Within five minutes, Meiring, the man who had interviewed him the day before, arrived and stuck a key in the lock.

'You're here bright and early,' he said. 'I like that.'

'Yes … thank you … I …'

'Find the place all right?'

'Yes, thank you.'

Meiring opened the door and entered, Luc followed diffidently, tongue-tied.

'You can sit here,' said Meiring, indicating a desk. 'I'll get you a cushion for that chair and a new blotter.'

'Thank you.'

Luc stood at the desk, uncertain whether to sit or not.

The others began to arrive. A young fellow in knitted cable-stitch pullover and sports jacket introduced himself as Rob Venter, and then introduced Luc to two typists, Marie and Estelle.

'Luc de Chalande?' echoed Estelle. 'What sort of name is that? What's your nationality?'

'I am French,' said Luc firmly.

Marie, however, merely nodded at him and took her place coolly at the desk next to his.

'Hmm ... hmmm ... a Latin lover,' giggled Estelle.

Luc pretended to be interested in what was in the drawers of his desk.

Until lunch-break, Luc worked on several forms that Meiring brought him and explained. From time to time he would glance across at the girl, Marie, but she ignored him stolidly. Then as he sat back to take his tea from the black man called the 'tea-boy,' he noticed her talking heatedly to Meiring. He watched them vaguely, without much interest, for their voices did not come through Meiring's glassed-in cubicle. After a while she returned to her seat, and Meiring motioned to Luc to come through to his office. Luc rose happily, expecting more work to be explained to him.

'Listen, De Chalande,' said Meiring. 'I'm going to move your desk to up here ... nearer to my cubicle. It won't make much difference. I hope you don't mind.'

'No ... no, not at all. If that is ... what is wanted.'

'Yes, yes ... just hang on here a minute. I'll call the tea-boy to move it.'

Meiring came back with the black man and the desk was moved up to a position slightly beyond the 'general office' allocated to the younger staff. Luc took his seat again, puzzled.

At one o'clock he made ready to leave the office, eager to see the lunch-hour streets and the shops. Rob Venter joined him on the sidewalk.

'Don't let it worry you,' he said.

'Worry me?'

'The move.'

'Oh that … oh no …'

'Dames are bloody mad, you know. Crazy.'

'I beg your …'

'That Marie Kruger. She really behaves like a "rock" sometimes.'

'I'm afraid I don't understand.'

'She behaves like a Dutchman. That's what we mean by "rock." She's hellavu narrow-minded and suspicious, you know, like a lot of Afrikaners. She only sticks to her own kind. Just as well. I'm sure none of us are interested in her. She'll put up with an English person, but Jews and Portuguese, never mind blacks and Coloureds, are out. She once told Estelle that if her father ever saw her talking to a Portuguese boy or a Jew, he'd break her neck.'

'Why are you telling me this?' Luc asked, but knew.

'Didn't you notice?'

'What?'

'That she complained to Meiring. Says you're Portuguese or Coloured and that she's not sitting next to you.'

'But I said … I'm French.'

'Well, she's too ignorant to understand the difference. Anyway don't let it worry you. And I hope you like living here. It's a great country, you know. We must get together some time, okay?'

'Okay,' said Luc.

He watched Rob's back as he turned and walked off, his sports coat flapping against his grey flannel trousers. Then he went to rest his forehead against a store-front. He wondered suddenly how Oncle Henri was getting on in Australia and he tried not to think of Maman and Papa fearfully waiting for him in their hotel room and hoping to hear the good news of his first day at work. Then Luc lifted his head and breathed deeply. There must be a way, he told himself; there must be a way to convince these people. He would find it.

SWEETNESS

Aftter keeping her mother four days in capricious labour, Clare chose to be born on January 29, 1914, the very day that Ghandi chose to leave South Africa for India, never to return. So on the night of January 29, Clare's mother, a sturdy eighteen-year-old, slept the sleep of exhaustion and disillusion, and General Smuts, rid of a troublesome mystic, slept the sleep of relief.

Clare's mother was Dutch, *her* mother, she always boasted, having twice met and talked with Queen Juliana of the Netherlands. The grandmother, the acquaintance of a queen, could substantiate her grandeur by showing her possessions: some fine old pieces of jewellery and crystal and a set of beautiful Dutch stamps, all of which, she said, she was saving for Clare. To Clare's unremitting disappointment and to her young mother's secret jealous satisfaction, a loitering miner out on strike stole the valuables from the grandmother's bedroom on the night of March 15, 1922, having first tied up the grandmother with her own Lyle Thread stockings. At eight years Clare received her first intimation that her childlike conviction of a foreordained distinction awaiting her might be misconceived.

Clare's father was a skinny Englishman with tired-lidded eyes and a cleft chin, a kind of watered-down working-class Douglas Fairbanks. He had come to Johannesburg to find a job on the mines, had married the stalwart Dutch girl several years his junior, and had proceeded to give her a baby every two years for the next twenty years, starting with Clare who had not wanted to be born. In return for these unwelcome favours, the Dutch girl perpetually fulminated and stormed at him, beat Clare cruelly with a rawhide whip kept hanging behind the kitchen door for that purpose, threw

15

cups and saucers at the walls, and on occasion was known to dump her husband's warm plate of dinner in his lap. When the tenth child was five, he died emaciated and disoriented, having been slowly strangled by the black lung contracted underground. Clare had loved her father. He never beat her unless her mother forced him to. She remembered once that he had spilled some sugar he was putting into his tea and how, under her mother's raucous impatience, he had winked at Clare and whispered, 'It's good sometimes to spill a little sweetness.'

Clare remembered that miners' strike of 1922, when her inheritance was stolen. When in 1984 the SABC ran a docudrama about it, Clare, now shrunken and ill, had felt herself to be more than usually tremulous. She suspected that the SABC was showing the movie for *her* specifically — that a public acknowledgement of her experiences might be the long-awaited distinction. She attended very closely to the TV images, would not allow her husband to talk during the show, and waited for the telephone to ring so that someone could question her on the veracity of something. Of course the phone did not ring, and of course Clare had known and knew very little about that huge disturbance. All she did recall was wandering out in the street when she heard shots in the distance and banging and shouting a few doors down. She saw Mr Koekemoer and Mr Luyt throw old furniture and woodslats into the street and thought they were angry. But when she saw Barnie Koekemoer and Boetie Luyt come out to help their dads, she was able to distinguish between violent ill-temper and urgent strategy. She went to help. Later, her mother, furious because Clare had 'interfered' with the neighbours, tied her right leg to the kitchen table with a length of rope and kept her there for two days, declaring that *that* would teach her to wander. For two days Clare had to crouch under the table at mealtimes and eat her food from a plate on the floor like a dog, keeping her eyes watchfully on the many legs surrounding her like jail bars in case someone inadvertently or on purpose kicked her.

As things turned out, there was no fighting on their street, but an unexploded bomb was dropped into their back garden, smashing several ripe pumpkins into a vast pink sticky pitted obscenity.

At seventy, trembling, Clare watched the SABC's show but would not admit to herself that the colours and significance of history had evaded her.

By the time she reached adulthood, Clare knew that the distinction she believed life would bestow on her would not come in the form of a grandmotherly gift, nor in the form of expansive motherly love, nor from her own energetic action, for her flesh and bones had been infused with a timidity akin to embalming fluid. Or rather, having lived for twenty-four years in the path of her mother's siroccos, her possible leaves and branches of enterprise had become schlerotic.

In 1938, hearing on the wireless names like Rhineland, Sudetenland, Czechoslovakia, and an infinite repetition of the opinions of Germany, Britain, France, and Russia, she grew to suspect that her distinction might come through travel, though each time she stared at a tiny hazy newsprint map she would feel the sensation of a rope tied round her right ankle. But she fantasized that someday someone would put a boat ticket into her hand, help her on board, and send her off somewhere.

That geographically expansive year of 1938 she met a daring blonde young goldminer, the owner of a monstrous Harley Davidson, part animal part machine. Every Saturday Wally the miner took her on the back of his bike to the bioscope and bought her a bag of chocolate creams. She would eat them all, not saving any for her grey-haired but still raving mother and her noisy siblings. And as the last one melted between tongue and soft-palate, she would think, *Sweetness, Sweetness.* In 1939 Wally and Clare married and

Clare felt (only momentarily, but not for the last time) that her bond with Wally might be her distinction. When Wally joined the army in 1942 to be part of the South African contingent of 'Tobruk Avengers', Clare realized enviously that she was still waiting for her own miraculous chance to travel — imaginary rope or no imaginary rope.

Wally returned from North Africa and Italy in 1945 an enthusiastic and unashamed drunkard. Brandy, sugar and water was his staple, the bread-and-butter of his imbibing, but he constantly experimented with other liquors and liqueurs, particularly on weekends. At one time it was eggnog and Kirsch that he mixed while extolling their strengthening properties, another it was Vodka laced with Kümmel, and for several months he went for 'kleiner-kleiners,' which are a shot of brandy swallowed fast followed by a more leisurely pint of beer. When he was trying out unusual mixtures or when he took to wine for a time, he would insist that Clare taste the drink to learn appreciation, and later offered the glass to the children, three little girls born in 1939, 1942, and 1946. In Italy, he maintained, the children drank wine and it was good for them. When the Nats got in in 1948 he made them all drink Van der Hum in celebration, even the two-year-old who then amused them all by dancing giddily.

The extended families on both sides deplored Wally's drunkenness openly. They all took turns to nag, coax, cajole, and threaten, and tried to shore up the sagging boughs of Clare's passivity so that she would stand against Wally's addiction. But she merely listened to their indignation, nodding and murmuring, but could not oblige them. What she did, however, was turn to the little girls. At bedtime she would tell them stories of her childhood and youth, of how her mother had mistreated her, and how neither happiness nor anything of distinction had ever come her way. She spoke slowly and softly. Hardly understanding her, the girls were nevertheless moved to a deep childish pity, and as the years went by they took more and more of the household tasks off her hands. And more and more, Clare discovered she had headaches, wonderful dank headaches that sent her to lie on a bed that metamorphosed into a darkened cave smelling of vinegar.

Her one consolation during those years of Wally's rowdiness and the wasting of his wages on drink was the vaguely bitter distinction she achieved by being the wife of a man of lost potential. Wally's family started the story that grew into an indestructible legend: that Wally had been a clever lad, and a bright young man, one who had been going to make a success of something some day, but that he would never do it now because of the drink. *Wally could have been a fine man and a good provider,* they would say to Clare, whereupon she would feel a mantle of dignity settle on her shoulders. Again she would nod and murmur, as if she had known all along of the potential, as if she had chosen her husband with acute discrimination.

As soon as they were old enough to get jobs, the three girls (variously glutted from having had to serve as parents to their parents) each left home in turn. Out in the world they hoped to rid themselves of a confused inner weightiness and to grow young, light, and easy. Eventually the eldest left for England and the two younger ones for Australia.

When the last girl left, Wally gave up drinking, not out of grief over losing his children but because he had been shocked sober by Prime Minister Verwoerd's assassination. He felt that the country now needed his full attention. He started learning Afrikaans — belatedly and badly. Clare, now fifty-two, found an uninebriate, politically muddled but verbose Wally very tedious. She hated to have the editorials from *Die Volksblad* read out to her in a halting Afrikaans which she did not understand even when it was unhalting.

She retreated more frequently into subterranean headaches. She also began answering more diligently the letters from her daughters. She suggested with increasing directness that she should visit them in turn, but either they did not comment on her suggestion or they kept pointing out that they had no place for a guest in their one-room apartments. Noleen, the eldest, salved her conscience each time she did not take up her mother's self-invitation by sending home parcels of good English chocolates. The word *Sweetness* still came to Clare as she ate them all, alone and methodically, but not as mellifluously as before. When her insistence that mothers and daughters should not be separated for too long became strident — she even underlined the words on the page — she merely succeeded in delaying her daughters' replies. Every day she visualized herself in a neat beige suit, carrying a fine leather overnight bag, boarding a large plane for London or Sydney. She saw herself as distinguished, even beautiful, as she crossed the expanse of an air terminal.

Over the years Clare grew smaller and more simian, though she was unaware of this. Whenever Wally took photos of her to send to her daughters, she would write behind them: *Supposed to be me! Supposed to be me!* Several times she argued that Kodak had sent back the wrong photos. During those years she once again enjoyed a dubious distinction, that of being married to the fittest old man in the neighbourhood. Wally had diverted all the enthusiasm he had felt for alcohol into personal fitness programmes. He had trimmed down, firmed up, and put on a healthy glow to his relatively unlined face. His once blonde hair had turned a brilliant admirable silver, and his long brisk walks around the neighbourhood earned him many acquaintances. Even the dogs seemed to like him. People she had never met stopped Clare at the shops, saying *Your husband is wonderful!* The family all said behind their hands, *Hasn't Clare aged?*

By 1976 when the Soweto riots broke out, the two daughters in Sydney had given Clare seven grandchildren between them, children she had only seen in bad reciprocal photographs, the sun in their eyes, all frowning, all blonde, all looking alike. Noleen in London had remained single, having had her fill of what Americans call nurturing (a word absurdly suggesting that human beings are as pleasant as gardens). Clare grew obsessed with the idea of visiting Noleen. As time passed, Noleen's spinsterhood made her age unnaturally in Clare's mind's eye until Noleen seemed her contemporary. She visualized them as two lone elegant women together in London. In the shops. In the parks.

In 1976 Wally gave up fitness for target practice. He also bought a thoroughbred Alsation which he named Lucia after a woman he had known in Italy. He had her spayed when she was still pre-estrous to make her wild, and took her to killer-training school. Clare hated Lucia. One day in 1979 Clare tripped over a rucked mat and fell, startling Lucia who promptly bit Clare several times in the head. The doctor who was called in to stitch the wounds was so appalled by the length and depth of the gashes that he notified the police. A magistrate ordered Wally to have Lucia destroyed but Wally's lawyer managed to get the sentence commuted to defanging. With a defanged Lucia back in the house even before Clare's bites were healed, she felt the first stirrings of an indignation rendered quiescent almost sixty years previously by her mother's rawhide whip. This little sprout of indignation pushed her to pack a suitcase and keep it in readiness under her bed.

By 1984 when the SABC broadcast its programme on the 1922 miners' strike, Lucia had been run over and Wally had had to have his bottom lip removed because of cancerous growths. He looked a little doglike himself without the lip but was still spry and shock-haired. He nattered all day in Afrikaans about two things only: the Great Depression and how he had retained his job, and his experiences in Cairo and Rome during the war. Clare never listened. But the two daughters from Sydney did visit that year, frightening Clare. They had both grown into stocky loudmouthed women, both uncannily like Clare's own mother. She would become dumb and wide-eyed in their presence. But her indignation was growing.

One spring morning, still in 1984, Clare went into town by bus. She withdrew a large sum of money from the savings account. Then she went by taxi to the South African Airways office and bought a return ticket for London. She had no intention of returning, but not wanting to get into a debate over legitimacy and sponsorship, she paid the fare. Using the same waiting taxi, she returned to Eloff Street where she bought an expensive beige suit from an exclusive boutique. Two weeks later she left the house silently at dawn while Wally was still asleep in his bed and walked to the corner phone-booth. There she phoned another taxi. As she was about to climb into the vehicle, she fell. She seemed to lie hazily on the sidewalk for a long time, but then with a lightened sensation and the awareness of bright sunshine, she was lifted up and driven away. She enjoyed gliding over the smooth tiles of the airport and with quiet excitement boarded the aircraft. There was a momentous roaring as it taxied down the runway. She was a little startled, however, when the stewardess who had been offering her candy to chew for take-off changed her uniform for a white coat and drew a syringe out of the air. Clare fell asleep with the strong sensation that there were ropes tying both her feet. When she woke much later and was introduced to a sweet-faced middle-aged woman named Noleen, she was convinced she had arrived.

THE CHANGE

At sunrise the backyard was like an ordinary box. The red brick walls on three sides squared off the red trampled earth on which no grass ever grew, and the roof of the north-east-facing house sent a rectangle of shadow over the back steps as if a lid were trying to come down or raise itself over the backyard. All shadows in the early morning were a uniform deep russet, and the sky was eggshell grey. An early riser might look upon the scene and wish that the mystery of uneven night might maintain itself indefinitely.

Before dawn the tokkalossie would leave, clicking like a rat across the concrete floor then shrinking to nothing and sliding like a sheet of grey paper under the door. Soon after a knife of sunlight would edge under the same door and Nomhla would know it was time to get up.

The kitchen in the main house would be gloomy and the surfaces cold to the touch in the thin winter light, but the air in the bedrooms would smell of open mouths and soft full intestines, and the sweetness of warm necks under sheets and blankets. Nomhla would boil water on the kitchen stove and set trays of tea to carry in to the sleepers.

That night the tokkalossie had tried galloping her home to the hills beyond Kwamandla, but she had clung to the mattress under her and flung her head heavily backward. There were nights when he rode and rode, twisting her this way and that, and then the hills would loom like bellies and buttocks crouched over her and she would give in, reaching down to hold his head.

Now Nomhla held her cardigan tight across her chest as she ran, head down, across the red earth of the backyard to the kitchen. Her pelvis and legs felt like sodden wood from the riding of the tokkalossie. When he was on top he pounded her as if she were new grain on the threshing floor; when she was on top she would bounce like a child on a loose bough until she would collapse forward, the tokkalossie taking, softly, her ear into his mouth.

All her things had always smelled of candle-wax: clothes, sheets, blankets, curtains. But she no longer smelled it. Now they reeked of the tokkalossie, and this she could smell: it was like the saliva of a dog or the feathers of fowl as the rain starts. The feet of her bed stood up on bricks, but still the tokkalossie found ways of leaping up on her, presenting himself like a large rat, a bullfrog, or a late summer's hare. Sometimes rarely he was a horned iguana and then she would have to cry out. Those were the nights she hoped Mrs Meintjies did not have curlers in her hair.

Nomhla was convinced that Mrs Meintjies never slept at all on the nights when she went to bed with curlers in her hair. The curlers must press into her head, giving her open-eyed hours to dwell angrily on all the corners that had tiny nests of tangled dust, on all the ceilings that had the pencil strokes of old cobwebs, all the stubborn blackness under pots, and the smudging inside her husband's collars. But surely, even awake, Mrs Meintjies could not hear the arrival of the tokkalossie right across the backyard in Nomhla's bedroom!

In the main house Mr Meintjies was sitting on the edge of his bed, his feet like beached fish planted wide apart on the floor, the toes moving. His stomach rounded onto his thick thighs, his chest with its small upright grey hairs drooping toward his stomach, and his head hung forward. His hands rubbed and rubbed his stubbly face. He ran fingers over his bare skull and picked at the edges of his nose. He yawned with a deep moan. He wondered whether it had been the barking of dogs or the arias of cats that had kept him restless during the night. Or the scuttling of rats. Or his wife's persistent sighs over an unattainable cleanliness.

'Where's the tea, Nomhla!' he called, his voice like cart-wheels over the gravel.

Nomhla poured boiling water on the tealeaves. Her palms felt as if she had been pressing them onto the stiff prickling tufts of burnt winter grass. The tokkalossie's head was like the hot blackened veld after a July fire. Beneath the stubble was a skull as hard as a kierie, out of which darted a tongue as fast as a lizard's, as bright as a flame.

In the second bedroom the five children opened their eyes and waited. The boys did not look at the girls and the girls ignored the boys. Nomhla would come in and give them each a mug of tepid tea which they would suck thirstily into their night-time throats, setting the five cups one after the other in age order back on the tray. Then the three girls would get up and go whispering to the bathroom. While they were out of the bedroom the two boys would dress. When the girls, still in their flannel nightgowns, came back to the bedroom, the boys would go to the bathroom. Down the centre of the bedroom floor was a thick chalk line drawn by Mrs Meintjies. No boy ever stepped over the line to the girls' side, and no girl ever trespassed across the chalk to the boys.

Until the bathroom was free of children. Mr Meintjies sat on the edge of his bed and drank three, four, five cups of tea, knowing that this was the best way to rinse the previous day's brandy out of his blood. Mrs Meintjies remained lying motionless in her own unruffled bed, staring at watermarks on the ceiling and seeing a straw hat with a ribbon and one glove and a powder puff. She would lie imperviously, staring at her mild creations, until her husband, hippopotamus-like from the back but priapic at the front, got up to wash.

Nomhla filled the kettle again to make more tea for breakfast. Then she began mixing the porridge. She had to stand patiently stirring and stirring it because if it had lumps the children pushed and pinched at her, hissing, lifting their small hard hands but not daring to slap or shout, so pushing, Nomhla, Nomhla, Nomhla. When the porridge pot was ready to set aside to keep warm, Nomhla cut twenty slices of bread for school lunches, cutting slowly and carefully so that the slices were neither thick nor uneven. On twenty slices she spread margarine, on two peanut-butter and syrup, on two sandwich-spread, on two cheese and jam, on two Marmite. Two were left plain. She placed ten margarine slices onto their mates and cut the sandwiches in half. Each child would find his or her two specific sandwiches and place them in a brown paper bag.

First the girls came in and then the boys, to take their places at opposite sides of the table to eat their porridge. The butter was passed, the sugar, and the jug of cream skimmed from the top of the milk. The girls spoke only to one another in lowered voices and throaty noises, and the boys shared the secrets of their minds and their pockets only with each other in undertone. Across the table malicious gleams and snide mouthings were exchanged in ordained silence. No one wanted the father's roar to bellow from the bathroom and beat upon the eardrums of offenders and non-offenders alike.

In the bathroom Mr Meintjies sounded like an elephant in a shallow pool. He noisily sniffed water up his nose, swallowed it gurgling towards his throat and then spat it out with force. He did this again and again, believing that in this way he could keep his passages open and his lungs healthy. The children left for school.

In a pink plush bathrobe Mrs Meintjies came to sit at the kitchen table, the curlers still punishing her head. Nomhla poured her a fresh cup of tea and put one egg in a pan to fry. 'Nomhla, I heard noises last night,' said Mrs Meintjies. 'I thought I heard noises again from your room.' Nomhla shook her head. *Haikona*, her head said, *Haikona*. No noises, Missis. Nomhla set the egg on a plate in front of

Mrs Meintjies. 'I don't want you letting boys come to your room, Nomhla,' said Mrs Meintjies regarding the egg. 'No Missis.' Mrs Meintjies would slice the white off in portions and eat it daintily until only the yolk remained. Then she would balance the whole soft yolk on her fork and drop it on her tongue like a communion wafer. Closing her mouth, her eyes glazing with pleasure, she would munch the yellow slowly with saliva and swallow it.

Mrs Meintjies went to take her bath. Round the edges of the bath she would leave a lacing of lilac-colored violet-smelling bath oil for Nomhla to clean off, and the waxiness of soap-scum. Mr Meintjies would leave the wash-basin criss-crossed with the trimmings of sideburns and nose-hairs.

When Mr Meintjies stamped into the kitchen, Nomhla set a slab of steak into the heated pan. Five minutes this side, five minutes that, one-two-three, Nomhla, don't over-cook. Seal in the juices. Mr Meintjies would chew his steak like an old buffalo chewing a cud, his eyes half closed, his shoulders hunched. Nomhla would stand at the stove, not watching. Steak upon steak over many years had decorated Mr Meintjies's arteries with deposits of pale fatty stalactites and stalagmites.

The kitchen no longer in use, Nomhla could cut her two doorsteps of bread, spread them with peach jam, pour a mug of cold tea and take her breakfast to eat on the back stairs. The sun would be up and the earth of the backyard a hard pink, the brick walls fibrous, and her own room fragile and tilting to one side. A brief gust could blow it over and expose her bed and her boxes and her picture of Lord Jesus and the candles stuck with wax onto saucers. Any light brighter than the dull oblong from her window would show the drying corpses of dead mice under her bed and the old thin black carapaces of cockroaches pressed beneath her trunk. And now the footprints of the tokkalossie scratched on her floor.

Nomhla knew her body was preparing itself not to bear children any longer and the preparations were like signs, on the air the hint of a dust-storm, or a fire, or far-off drum-beats. The tokkalossie received the messages and came maliciously titupping under the door, keeping to the shadows, and then leaping onto her. In his mischief he would want to challenge the signs, forcing her to conceive again or, thwarted, jockeying her into her ancestors' cairns beyond Kwamandla.

Disturbed, Nomhla ate and drank and then returned to the house. As she washed her mug and plate she once again felt the pain in her pelvis as though the tokkalossie had stoked warm coals into her that now had cooled and grown heavy.

Mrs Meintjies put on a pink dress, powdered her face, and unwound the curlers. She brushed and brushed at her hair, hurting her scalp, dissatisfied, as she had been for the past five years, with this mass of greying fibres that would not conform to any picture of a woman's hairstyle that she had ever studied. She felt an obscure anger, suspecting that her husband was to blame for her hair's disobedience. And, indeed, the following year, when Mr Meintjies collapsed and died, her hair began to relax and thin out and she was comforted. Mrs Meintjies would make a good widow.

While Mrs Meintjies was at the shops, Nomhla washed and dried dishes, scrubbed the kitchen floor, vacuumed the living-room, swept the bedrooms and made the seven beds, scoured the bathroom, dusted, and began ironing the previous day's washing. At three o'clock she again took two slices of bread and jam and a mug of tea and went to her room. But she could not eat. She drank the tea, straightened her bed, and without removing her headscarf and shoes lay down on the cover. Soon she dozed, dreaming of a buzzing peacefulness, as if she were a child resting in the motionless sunlight of Kwamandla while wasps worked busily at a new nest under the thatch.

The little boys came home from school. They changed into khaki pants and shirts and old jerseys, and grew absorbed in scraping a network of roads in the dry dirt of the backyard over which they ran small cars and trucks, mumbling through pursed lips brimm, brimm, brimm ...

Both good, contained little boys, with their lowered voices and small movements, were nurturing in their hearts the seeds of an enormous cruelty that at a future time would devastate two families. But now they forced themselves to be good and went calling, 'Nomhla, Nomhla, Nomhla, come help!' Their mother was trying to get through the front gate while carrying heavy shopping bags. Nomhla sat up groggily.

Straightening her head scarf and hugging her cardigan to her, Nomhla went running, head down, up the side of the house, the little boys after her. She and they took packages from Mrs Meintjies who watched frowning, her tired voice warning them to take care not to crack the eggs, not to squash the bread out of shape or cause the tomatoes to burst, not to clang the bottles together dangerously, and not to let the string bag of potatoes break. The little boys thought their mother was reading their minds: they hoped to see dusty brown imperfect potatoes go rolling across the paving stones, to be kicked and dived at and tossed to each other.

In the kitchen Mrs Meintjies unpacked the groceries, pushing towards Nomhla the things she was to cook for dinner. 'Tea, Nomhla, tea,' said Mrs Meintjies yawning. Her yawn stretched, showing the wagging pink of her open throat. 'I don't get enough sleep,' she said.

Kettle in hand, Nomhla nearly spilled water as she asked herself for the first time whether there was a tokkalossie that visited white girls and women, whether he might sidle into the children's room and slip into bed with the oldest girl, causing an unexpected and probably bewitched grandchild to be bestowed upon Mr and Mrs Meintjies in nine months' time, or whether on moonless nights he slunk into Mrs Meintjies's smooth unstirred bed, slyly keeping it unstirred as he covered her carefully with himself, now flattened like a soft woollen blanket, his plump mushrooming penis nodding gently against her sleeping pubis. The white tokkalossie would not assume the shape of a rat or cat, a hare or a leopard. No, he would be like a book or ghost stories read last thing at night, or vibrant, evaporating brandy in a glass for sleeplessness, or a hotwater bottle losing its water in a widening pool.

Nomhla made beef stew, mashed potatoes, pumpkin, and green beans for dinner. She sliced beets and sprinkled them with sugar and vinegar. She made an egg custard, stirring, stirring to keep it smooth. And she put on a pot of puto for herself. As he took his place gruntingly at the head of the table, Mr Meintjies said, not looking at Nomhla, 'You mustn't let boys come to your room at night.' But he said the words as if he had been told to but did not believe there were such boys who still came visiting. 'I want peace and quiet at night,' said Mrs Meintjies sharply, looking into Nomhla's eyes, then quickly looking down at her plate. She hoped suddenly but obscurely that Nomhla had poisoned the food. Nomhla looked into the eyes of the oldest girl. They were blank and heavy-lidded as if she were enthralled by the deep dream she had entered. But the little boys' eyes were bright as they wondered whether they could kick the little girls without being detected and accused. The little girls, eyes alert, looked hard into the little boys' faces, daring.

Later in her room, Nomhla set her candles on a crate so that they might compose large hilly shadows in her room, and placed a little pot of water on her Primus stove to make her own tea freshly. She looked forward to feeling the stiff crumbling cornmeal on her fingers as she scooped it from pot to mouth, and the saltiness of the meat gravy on her tongue. She would eat and then get a kettle of hot water from the kitchen to wash her arms and neck with. Then at last she could get under the blankets and stretch her tired body. If the tokkalossie came swirling in under her door like a spring wind, she would lie quietly and let him knead her like yeast bread and take her, rising, in the heat of his breath.

Mr Meintjies was pouring his last brandy of the evening with a thick unsteady hand while Mrs Meintjies sat at her dressing table looking at her hair. 'That Nomhla is getting strange,' she said, 'and she smells. Maybe we should get another girl and let her go.' Mr Meintjies did not answer. His wife had said the same thing at least once a month for the past fifteen years. He made the brandy a stiff one and watched it shake like liquid garnets in the glass. Neither knew that at that moment Nomhla was speeding comet-like over the house, skewered by the tokkalossie, flaming to the hills beyond Kwamandla.

OFAY-MAJOOR

Places like Elandsheuwel must be home to many, many people, millions probably. Since I got a salary increase and could buy a TV set, I've seen a lot of places on the box that look just like Elandsheuwel. The Australian flatlands look like one hell of a big Elandsheuwel. Places like Provo, Utah (I saw that in *The Executioner's Song*) look like Elandsheuwel. You know, dry, flat country, poverty, soil erosion, and the cheap buildings all looking temporary, as if they don't belong on the earth. Bloegomdal, our township just outside Elandsheuwel, looks as if it would need just one medium-sized tornado to blow all the square boxes away. If a wind like a big giant hand could come and sweep it up, throwing us humans into outer space, then the rough veld could spread itself evenly and without wounds to the horizons, all the smoke from the township and the old shunting yards could disappear, and the sky could come out blue and clear even where the main town once stood. I've seen pictures of parts of Nigeria that look like Elandsheuwel, and even parts of Sicily. There must be more of them, in the Soviet Union, for instance.

I suppose I shouldn't mind the place seeing that there are so many people in the world that have to live in identical spots. But it's bitterly cold in the winter. Some days the wind roughens and shrinks the skin of my hands and face and burns inside my nostrils as I do my rounds. The grass, where there is grass, is dull and yellow, and easily set alight.

In the winter there is not much pleasure for the eye anywhere. The darkness falls early and the smoke hangs more heavily over the iron roofs of the township than at any other time of the year. All night I can hear the neighbour's children coughing. When we get those terribly cold spells, with snow on the mountains, old people die from cold.

In the summer the town can get so hot that some of the chickens the people keep collapse in the dirt. And old people die of the heat. I remember how the Bakkes's house in Voortrekker Street, in the white part of town, got a huge crack one summer down the plateglass front window. The weather had been still and hot and without rain for two weeks, and Mrs Bakkes said that their living-room used to bake like a kiln. One afternoon, old man Bakkes was watering his flowers at the gate when he decided to train the hose over the front window, thinking to cool the living-room off. But the glass was so hot that when the cold water burst onto it, it cracked. It remained like that until the day the old lady died and the old man was taken away by his daughter to Johannesburg and new people moved in.

I've been delivering mail for seven years now in the Elandsheuwel district and I've got to know the people pretty well, including the old people that live in the 'Military Pension' houses along Voortrekker Street. Some of them live funny lives, it seems to me. Aunt Marnie started off with three cats. Now, I don't know how many she's got and I don't think she knows. She says that she has got a reputation as a cat-lover so folks who don't want their cats any more or get litters of kittens they can't be bothered with, come in the night and drop the animals over Aunt Marnie's fence. She hasn't got the heart to send any of them to the SPCA. Letta Manko (her late-husband was a Polish soldier who came to South Africa after the war) does not want to admit that she is a pensioner. She used to be a gymnastics teacher and is still very thin and wiry. She takes a daily ride on her ten-speed bike and sometimes I see her going down the highway, upright in the saddle, hands at her hips, grey hair breezing backwards, happy in the feeling that she is still young. I hope her reflexes are good. This town is full of punks whose two interests are beer-drinking and zooped-up grumbling cars.

Then there is Sergeant-Major Bakkes and his wife and their cracked front window. He started calling me 'Klonkie' when I first took the job, and even though I'm twenty-three now and have been given a decent bike, Klonkie is the name he gives me. I call him 'Ofay-majoor.' Either he doesn't understand the word 'Ofay' and isn't interested in asking me its meaning, or he understands and doesn't care. But frankly, I think that most of the time he doesn't hear me address him. He never listens much to anyone; only to himself.

Usually Mrs Bakkes waits for me at the gate, though sometimes, if the sergeant-major is busy in the garden she retreats to the front door in the shade, away from his lecturing. His tongue is never still. I suppose I am an important regular event, one of the few outsiders they see. Their children write often and send presents, but they don't seem to want to visit. Probably because of the old ofay-majoor.

In the summer, the houses along Voortrekker Street smell of mown grass and wet earth, especially the Bakkes's place where the long narrow garden is well-kempt and well-watered, and Mr Bakkes's vegetables and flowers are like showpieces. He says there is nothing better for you than fresh carrots, tomatoes and lettuce, straight from the garden. If we ate those every day, we wouldn't need medicines. In the autumn, he looks a bit miserable as he rakes up the leaves and starts growing cauliflowers, a vegetable he doesn't fancy much. But no matter the time of the year, he always talks about his health.

'Ag, Klonkie, I'm as fit as a fiddle,' he said to me one morning when I stopped to admire his garden. It was during the warm winter of eighty-one when people were growing strawberries in June, large pale pinkish fruit nestling under the leaves in the light-coloured sand of our region. 'Look, I can't ride a bike, but I do breathing exercises when I get up,' he said, showing me how he inhaled and how broad he could expand his chest, 'and I can walk briskly still.' He strode a few steps up the path. Mrs Bakkes had come to the door to see what mail there was. 'Not like my wife. She's walking like a real old auntie these days,' he mocked. 'And look at her boeppens. Hold in your boeppens, Tannie ...'

'Liefie, don't talk like that in front of a postman,' she said. I knew she was going to say *Coloured* but stopped herself.

'Ag, Tannie, what does he care?' jeered the old man.

'When you're getting on and your children are grown, you have a right to have a big stomach, ney Merrem,' I said, feeling sorry for her.

'There's not a damn thing wrong with *me*,' said the ofay-majoor, striding down the path again. 'Klonkie, I'm as strong as an ox, except for this eye.' He stuck his face toward me, indicating his right eye which did seem blurred and not focusing, the pale blue and pink-rimmed eye of a fair old person, small and piglike, and repulsive to me. 'They'll have to shoot this old boy to get rid of him,' he crowed. His wife, grey and haggard, was watching him silently from the front stoep, her hands folded across her belly. She tried winking at me.

'Maarsers going to live to be a hunnert,' I said, as was expected, winking too.

Then I had my two weeks' annual leave and went to see my parents at Elsiesrivier. On the first day of my return to work, it looked as if there was no one home at the Bakkes's house. But Aunt Marnie told me that Mrs Bakkes had had a stroke a couple of days before and was in the hospital. Apparently she had been drying her hair with an electric dryer plugged into a light socket when she passed out. The sergeant-major saw her falling and thought she had electrocuted herself. He didn't know what to do at first. He switched off the dryer and then began phoning doctors. He had to phone no less than four before he could get one to come out and bring an ambulance.

'Ja, things are not easy these days with doctors, Mr Wouter, even for us whites,' said Aunt Marnie.

Anyway, Mrs Bakkes was recovering slowly and the sergeant-major was at the hospital every day, feeding her himself, now that she was off the intravenous, and trying to teach her to talk again. It seemed to me that he would be good at teaching talking. When I saw him again a few weeks later in his garden, he told me about it.

'God, Klonkie, I had the bladdy fright of my life. There she lay, mouth open like a cup, legs apart, just as if she'd died. And what a weight! I couldn't move her, and I'm strong, hey. Those bladdy hair-dryers are no good, I say. Man, they heat the scalp, it's obvious. So I've made her have her hair cut, short-short, like a boy's, so no more using those bladdy dangerous things.' He turned to look half-guiltily at his wife who had come to stand in the doorway. But now she had to hold onto the jamb and I could see that her whole body trembled. Her hair was cropped off like some poor old lag. She mumbled something.

'What's the Merrem say, Ofay-majoor?' I asked.

'Ag, man, she's complaining that she hates her hair. But I don't take any notice. And Tannie,' he said, turning to her, grinning maliciously and yet also as if he were afraid, 'Tannie, don't go mumbo-jumbo, goo-goo-goo, like that. Speak *properly*, man!'

More and more letters and parcels came now that the old woman was not well, but I never saw any of the daughters they said they had. I noticed as the weeks went by that Mrs Bakkes's speech improved, but she still spoke slowly, like a child with porridge in its mouth. Yes, she reminded me of a child, what with the short hair and the bones of her neck shining whitely just under the skin. Her eyes were also very bright, showing all the anger she could not spit out because her tongue was too slow. She would stagger down the path when she saw me coming, trying to get to me before the old man did, to tell me things. 'I'm like a prisoner in this house, Mr Wouter,' she told me one Saturday. 'He won't even let me walk to the shops on my own but he has to walk with me, ordering me all the time. He won't take me on any trips, not even to see my daughters, because, excuse me, you see I have to make several visits to the toilet while we're on the road. He hates to stop once he's in the car, he must get to the other end as quickly as possible. What's the rush, I say?'

'Ah, that's too bad,' I said.

'He says that if I'll sit on the back seat and keep, excuse me, a chamber pot with me to use when I need to, we can go somewhere. But I can't do that. I would be too embarrassed to empty the pot when we arrived.'

'Ag, Merrem, how can he ask that?'

'You know, I would not wish a stroke on my worst enemy,' she added, and I wondered how this shivering old woman could have had an enemy at all, unless it was the ofay-majoor. 'The pain in your head and stomach is something awful. The wires, you know, that they put in you, make your stomach bloat like a ball and you can't move because of all the pipes, and your back feels like iron.'

'Haai, that's not good.'

'You must cut down on salt, Mr Wouter, and not get yourself worried about things,' she advised me.

'I kannie worry about nothing, Mrs Bakkes. Only the dogs that want always to be biting me,' I said, speaking like the klonkie all those people liked me to be.

Eventually, some months later, I saw one of the daughters. She came down from Johannesburg because her mother had had another stroke, but this time the old man had a dose of 'flu — so much for his bakgat health — and could not sit at his wife's bedside and help out. The daughter was a little thing with frizzed blonde hair, blue eyes just like the old man, and a low wide flat bottom covered in Italian-style pants, the kind that puff out and then come tight at the ankle. She had driven up to the front gate in her Mercedes just as I was peddling up the road and Letta Manko was whizzing down it, her face averted. Miz Manko doesn't want to see the evidence of sickness, says Aunt Marnie. The sergeant-major was waiting for his daughter.

'Those darn nurses. They have the eyevee going too fast,' I heard her say as I parked my bike. 'No wonder Mom's stomach was hurting her. I made them slow it down and got them to turn her on her side so I could rub her back. She was in agony. I don't know why she doesn't speak up. But those stupid nurses piss me off too.'

'You mustn't swear like that, Desiree,' said the old man, shocked but subdued.

'Well they make me sick. When I wanted to leave, Mom got hysterical and started plucking all the tubes out and crying, and I could she was infuriating the matron. The way she glared! But no damn sympathy. Anyway, I calmed Mom down and stayed on a bit. I'll go back after I've had a clean-up and something to eat.' The young woman stalked into the house like an angry old ruffled hen.

'I think my old lady's going mad,' said the Ofay-majoor softly to me, looking confused. He blew his nose, tried inhaling deeply, but only ended up coughing.

'I get so worried about that old girl, Klonkie,' he said to me the next day. 'Why does she keep keeling over like that?'

'Man, I can't say, Ofay-majoor. I think that veins in the head are like brick walls or rather dam walls. If there's too much pressing on them for too long, they just give in.'

'Even with this 'flu, I'm pikfyn, you know, Klonkie. Exercise and diet is what does it. My wife doesn't exercise and she doesn't eat right. For breakfast I have a handful of muesli, for lunch vegetables from the garden, and for dinner just a bit of stew with the fat scooped off. As you said, I'm going to live to be a hundred,' he added, nodding his head. He inflated his chest and exhaled slowly, carefully. I noticed that his pants were getting big for him and empty behind as if his flesh was drying up. And his old jersey hung loose around his shoulders.

But he was pleased with himself, that old man. Nothing hindered him. He wasn't even embarrassed when one Saturday afternoon I walked right up to the front door because he wasn't at the gate to accept a parcel and caught him in his hat. It was a hot September day and the door stood wide open. I could see him sitting in an armchair watching the television, but was surprised to see that he had a large straw hat with the crown pulled right over his face. I thought he was asleep, so I knocked loudly. 'Die pos is hier,' I said. He pulled the hat off and got up. 'Were you sleeping?' I asked.

'No, don't be stupid, Klonkie. I never sleep when western province is playing northern, the last game of the season. It's just my eye. You know, I found that if I pull the hat down over my face like this,' he showed me, 'and look through the little holes in the weave;' I could see his eyes blinking through the criss-crossing of the straw; 'I can see the television better. Now that I've discovered this, I don't think I'm even going to bother to wear glasses. This old boy doesn't need four eyes yet!'

'Isn't it hot and horrible sitting with a straw hat over your face?'

'No, man, Klonkie, I can see good like that!'

'Ofay, I learn something new every day,' I said, giving him the parcel. 'When I'm old I'll get myself a hat like that.'

'What do you mean *old?* I am not *old,*' he said.

When Mrs Bakkes got out of hospital, she walked and talked even slower than before. She never waited at the gate for me any more, so I used to go right up to the front step.

Her hands would shake as if her bones were their own masters, moving themselves as they wanted, and her head would nod as if she were agreeing to everything in the world, while all the time she was protesting: I could see it in her eyes. Her bits of hair were not totally white, yet, strangely, she had started looking younger ... in a fierce sort of way. Her flesh was holding tighter against the bones of her face, and it was spare, almost smooth, as if returning her, now at the end, to her girlhood. Her face was very unlike the old sergeant-major's kisser, which although it had never grown wise, was dissolving like that of a wax baby-doll in the sun. His little eyes and his pink lower lip looked as if they were surprised by these events of old age.

One day when the door stood wide open and the sitting room was empty, I did something I had never done before — I stepped inside. 'Hey, mense,' I said, 'come and get it!' At first there was no sound, then I saw Mrs Bakkes helping herself down the stairs, bouncing slowly down on her bum, just like a toddler. Carefully, spiderly, she crawled down.

'Is Merrem all right?' I asked, walking forward to help her. But the old man came out of the kitchen door at the side.

'Hey, Klonkie, you have no right to come in here,' he said sharply.

'I don't want to come into any white house, Ofay,' I said. 'I thought your wife needed help. She can't walk ...'

'Oh she can walk all right. But she can't manage the stairs very well, so she has to crawl up and down. It does her good. Exercise is what she needs. Those stairs are the best thing that could've happened to her, I say.' I wasn't so sure. As I stepped outside the old woman sat on the bottom step to get her breath.

'Isn't it for heart trouble that you must do a little exercise? Not for strokes?' I asked. I remember how my father had had a heart attack soon after my brother got arrested for

I.D.B. My sister used to have to take Pappie on walks though she hated it because all he would do was moan that my brother had got himself purposely arrested so that his father would have a heart attack. Which wasn't true. My bro was terrified of jail.

'For everything, for everything,' insisted the Ofay-majoor. 'Jong, I know what's good and what isn't good. I look after her like a Dutch uncle. I know when and what medicines she must take. Since you've already put your foot in here, you may as well come right in and see,' he said, motioning me toward a chest of drawers. 'See, these bottles are her medicines. Three of these green capsules in the morning, two of these yellow ones before lunch, and all five at bedtime, including a little sleeping tablet. But I try to give her only half of the sleeping tablet.'

'Man, the doctor said I could have a whole one,' said the old woman very slowly, slurring, but her eyes were sharp.

'But Tannie, it's not good for you,' pleaded the sergeant-major.

'The doctor said …'

'Nevermind. And here, Klonkie, are my tablets. The doctors are always giving me pills for this and pills for that, but I never take them. I don't trust them. Here … they gave me these antibiotics for my ear.' I saw now that the old man had cotton-wool stuffed in his left ear. 'But I only took two of them. If *two* can't work, then I don't want the rest.'

I tell you, the man had dozens of bottles neatly arranged in the chest of drawers. Enough to start his own little chemist's shop. I wondered why he kept going to the doctors and getting treatment if he didn't want the pills.

'And look here,' he interrupted my thoughts, opening another drawer. 'I've got eye-glasses for life.' He pointed to seven sets of spectacles, each in its own case. 'They keep prescribing glasses for me, but I don't wear them. But why should I care? If they want to prescribe them, let them. The army pays. Why, I haven't paid a penny for all her hospitals and everything,' he said, turning proudly to his wife. 'It must have run into thousands by now …'

He pulled himself upright and ran his hands through his own long white hair. 'Do you want a pair of glasses, Klonkie?' he asked slyly.

'Ag no, Maarser. What must I do wif glasses?' I played along.

'You can give them to your mother or father.'

'No, Maarser. They've bof got glasses.'

'How old are they?'

'Ofay, man, they're younger than you, hey,' I replied, also slyly. He was pleased.

'Klonkie, if you get yourself in trouble and need anti-biotics, you can come to me,' he said, laughing. I laughed too, putting the letters into the old woman's trembling hands. She made a noise, either trying to laugh or wanting to speak, but he babbled on.

Then one Friday evening some months later, I was sitting over a couple of beers and the local newspaper when I read that Alida Marie Bakkes, wife of former Sergeant-Major Gordon Bakkes, had died and was being buried that Saturday coming. The next morning I rode my bike up Voortrekker Street and could see all the Mercedes and BMWs and Porsches parked around. I took Aunt Marnie's mail right up to her door.

'Merrem Aunt Marnie, what happened?' I asked.

What she told me was sad but not so unexpected if you think about it. The Ofay-majoor had taken his wife to the doctor on the Wednesday and the doctor had said that she was doing very well indeed. He gave her a new prescription for sleeping pills and said she could even take two of that particular kind quite safely if she found that one did not help her to sleep. But that night the Ofay-majoor insisted that she could only have half a tablet. So, she must have pretended to be asleep when he came in to look at her in bed before going to his room, as he did every night, because it seems she got up in the dark and crawled downstairs to the chest of drawers and took the whole bottle of tablets with a glass of brandy.

I decided to get my work done quickly, get off early, and go to Mrs Bakkes's funeral, even if only to the church. I really felt pity for that old woman and a kind of admiration that she didn't let that old man sergeant-major her to the end. I suppose I felt sorry for the old man too, though what he did at the funeral still has me aggravated.

He was wearing full military dress, with all his ribbons and medals and things, but over the last few years his body had shrunk and the uniform was too big for him. His face was very swollen from crying, but instead of sitting quietly with his daughter, he kept turning in his seat to see who had come to his wife's funeral. Though I'd be surprised if he could see much because he didn't have his glasses on. Maybe it was just numbers he was interested in.

When he saw me, he made a movement with his hand as if to wave me away. I just nodded to him. Blow me down, if he didn't get up from his pew, even though his daughter tried to stop him, and come over to where I was sitting, minding my own business, listening to the organ music, and waiting for the minister to begin.

'Hey, Klonkie, you can't come to a *white* person's funeral,' he whispered hoarsely to me, his red eyes peering down. I folded my arms.

'Don't talk shit, Ofay,' I whispered back. 'I'm allowed in this church any time I want. The Methodists have been letting us Klonkies in for years now, didn't you notice?'

He looked as if he wanted to hit me.

'Don't worry, Ofay, I won't come to *your* funeral,' I assured him.

He looked around the church a bit uncertainly, but when

he saw that no one was paying him particular attention, except for his daughter, who was staring, he tiptoed, hunched over, back to his seat.

I never saw the Ofay-majoor again. He had to go and live with that daughter in Johannesburg. My cousin who has a clerical job in the Elandsheuwel Military Camp where old Bakkes used to be stationed says he heard from a telephone operator at the Witwatersrand Command that Sergeant-Major Gordon Bakkes shot himself with his military pistol. It seems he hated living in the townhouse with his daughter and her husband, and even though he nagged day in and day out, they would not let him make a vegetable garden in the grounds. So he called it a day. Just like that.

This winter is very harsh. We have had snow and burning frost. Letta Manka hasn't been riding her bike, and the town authorities have made Aunt Marnie put away all but two of her cats. In the Bakkes's house a new pensioned couple have moved in. They have a sign up at the gate saying 'hand-made jerseys for sale.' Whenever I bring their mail up to the door, I see them both sitting, concentrating hard, at knitting machines. I am placing an order for a beige vee-neck jersey.

ZACHARIAS

Zack

The security guard hurt my arm so bad. Wrenched a muscle, it feels like. It's hard anytime to keep this bicycle going straight, but now I'm having a lot of trouble holding the handlebars steady, what with the pain like a hot knife slicing up and down my bone, and my throat dry from the shame of it all. I should've waited for Joey to drive me to the shops in his skedonk, but he was late and I needed to buy the right-sized screwdriver to fix the loose outlet in my room, and you can never find a decent tool in its place anymore in that house. So I took my bike. But I got distracted in True Value's, I always do, they got so much stuff. Every day of the week someone must be inventing a new tool or gadget or thing, seems to me. I like browsing up and down the rows more than anything, being surprised by other people's good ideas. I even love the smell of a hardware store, fresh paint, clean steel, new oil, and the strange dry smell of plastic containers. I wish I owned a hardware store. That's probably what I should've done when I was young, got myself a hardware store instead of joining the navy and getting myself shipped out to so many places that all places became the same place to me. No point in moaning now. And as the Buddha might say, all places and things are part of the Good.

So I sort of lost myself examining the new sanders they had in and the cans of liquid nails and rust inhibitors. Then I saw these new little voltage converters, the kind you take with you to foreign countries for your hair-dryer or shaver. In my day they used to be big and heavy as a spanner, but now you can buy one that weighs nothing and is only about two by two by four. Except that they cost. The one I bounced in my hand cost near fifty rands. Then my mind

47

went hazy again and I couldn't remember what I'd come to buy. I walked up and down, and the rows of things were blurring into floating colours, so I decided to go across to the café to get a cup of coffee to shake me back into myself. But as I left the store an assistant and a security guard stopped me and asked me what I had in my hand, and, ag jinna, it was that little converter. I handed it back to the clerk saying, Holy Moses, I'm sorry, man, I forgot I had that! But as I turned to go the security guard grabbed me by my left arm and I don't know what got into me but I tried to pull away and, before I knew it, I'd lifted my fists. Then he got a real good hold of me and twisted my arm behind my back. And all of a sudden there were people come to watch, and he doubled me forward, and I was panting and feeling my face going purple and the sweat prickling out, looking true-as-God like a thief. So then he pushed me ahead of him through the True Value again to a back room and another officer came to help him take a statement. But lucky for me old Frank Bezuidenhout the owner came in from lunch or wherever and he said he knew me for a long time and wasn't going to lay a charge. So they let me go and, feeling like a thief and the tears and saliva pouring down the back of my throat, I walked past the people, many staring at me I think, though I couldn't see clearly. I got my bike out of the rack and now I'm going home. But the shame makes it seem as if I'm pedalling through heavy sand and the walls and gates along this stretch don't look familiar anymore.

Uncle Zackie

Had I not come home when I did, Uncle Zackie would be dead now, his thin old body lying in a body-bag on the ambulance stretcher and him not sitting in a lotus position in his bed, his mind trying to get steady from the meditation, I suppose, even if he is trembling.

I'd told him I'd take him shopping this afternoon but soccer practice went on longer than usual. I drove home as fast as I dared, knowing there was always a cop-car lurking under the trees on Suzman Avenue, and as I was about to run inside, I caught a glimpse of movement among the blue gums out the back. I looked again and saw Uncle Zackie standing on an upended apple-crate with one end of a piece of rope around his neck, busy tying the other end over a hefty branch. Even now I can't believe I acted as quickly as I did. But I think at the back of my mind there has always been a voice telling me that someday sooner or later I'd have to act fast on Uncle Zackie's behalf. I dashed indoors, grabbed a sharp kitchen knife, shot out again, got the apple-crate back on its side, jumped up and, supporting Uncle Zackie's gurgling body, sawed through the rope. He was too heavy for me to keep hold of so I had to let him fall, and he lay writhing and marching with his feet as if he wanted to walk away from his life. I immediately eased the knot he'd tied at his left ear and tugged the rope off. He'd scoured the skin off his under-jaw, leaving a jagged red mark, worse than a burn, and minute drops of blood were already forming on it. As he sucked in air noisily, I checked him for broken bones but there were none. So I got behind him and helped him to a sitting position.

'Why'd you cut me down, hey Joey?' he wheezed, swallowing, swallowing.

'Don't talk stupid,' I said, taking hold of his left arm to help him get to his feet.

'The other arm, the other arm,' he cried.

So I got his right arm draped over my shoulder and got him up. His soles scrambled against the earth as if he was drunk, but then he seemed to get a firmer foothold. I helped him indoors and to his room. But he wouldn't lie down.

'I'll just sit here … like this and … get back into myself,' he said in his low mild voice, climbing shakily onto the bed and arranging himself in that position he learned from some Buddhist monk when he was in Japan. 'I've had a terrible blow to my self-pride, Joey ...'

'And what about your body, Uncle Zackie? What about your jaw? Just look at it! Don't you want to get some kind of ointment?'

'In a little while, okay,' he whispered.

'Don't you want to explain to me what happened, why you ...?'

'Later, my boy, later.' He closed his eyes and slowly dismissed me by lifting his hands, palms together, to his nose, fingers straight. I hung around for a minute and then went to the living-room. There I got the shakes myself and began dry sobbing.

Now, although I'm not supposed to touch my parents' booze, I'm sipping a stiff tot of Glenlivet to calm myself down and help me think about what I'm expected to do next and what I'm supposed to say to my folks.

My brother Zack

He's one of those eccentric bachelors some families have to put up with. They're like cheerful skeletons that won't stay put in their assigned cupboards. They never act normally, they dress needlessly unfashionably (my brother doesn't *have* to buy clothes from the second-hand store on Hendrik Verwoerd), and they have a penchant for saying the wrong things at the wrong time. They are the sort of people their families don't like to invite to weddings or bar mitzvahs or reunions because they make everyone feel guilty for celebrating too lavishly or too loudly. I do love my brother, and Basil, my husband, doesn't really mind him, but there are times when we wish he didn't have to live with us. But he can't live alone anymore, and he has nowhere else to go. Most of the time he's no trouble. These days he makes no noise to speak of and he spends his time doing little repair jobs, reading hardware catalogues, riding his bike to wherever he wants to go, and doing his meditating.

He used to be quite wild when he was young. In fact, he was rather nice-looking and I had something of a schoolgirl crush on him. Why, I remember when he was in matric he punched a teacher who was tormenting some kid, and he got himself expelled for that. My dad then insisted that he join the navy which he did and got himself shipped off to the Far East. He wrote to Mom, poor boy, that he was seasick all the time and had to carry a small bucket around with him as he went about his duties. So some of the other chaps started calling him *Emmertjie*. Then one night, apparently, when he was on shore leave in Pusan, Zack saw an officer slap an enlisted man in the face and he jumped in, throwing punches. Soon there was a regular street-brawl between the officers and men. He was arrested and sent to the guard-house or lockup, or wherever it is they put sailors.

After that he experienced some kind of Eastern religious conversion or other, and he became more subdued. By the time he was discharged from the navy in seventy-four he saw himself as something of a mystic but to me he was, frankly, just an annoying kind of do-gooder. For the next fifteen years, until he came to live with us, he never held a normal job. Oh, he always worked, don't get me wrong: Joe's no slouch. He's been a janitor-cum-night watchman at the old synagogue in Joubert Park and they let him live in the basement of the building, a large gloomy dank room still with a dirt floor. I'm not making this up! Then he ran a soup-kitchen in Westdene where he sometimes had to protect the food and equipment with his fists. He has driven a truck for St Vincent de Paul's; he helped to organize blanket and food relief in Alexandria township during the heavy floods of eighty-one; and then he moved to Durban for a while where he was a cook at the Seamen's Mission on Point Road where he claims he had occasion to use his fists protecting the old and the weak. But I don't believe him: he was getting too old himself by that stage. The year before Mom died, she said to me, 'Ruth, your brother is a Hasid.'

'Mom,' I said, 'you're talking nonsense. That man's always getting himself into fights. Is that what Hasidim do?'

'Yes, as a matter of fact. If you knew any Jewish history you'd know that in the past they would often have to settle arguments physically.'

But my mother was making this up: she knew precious little Jewish history herself. Invention obviously runs in my family.

'Why doesn't he get himself a proper job, Mom? All his jobs are so … so low class.'

'Ruth, Hillel was a woodcutter and Shammai a carpenter.'

What could I say?

In eighty-eight, after Zack had been so ill with pneumonia, we insisted he come and live with us. Joey was pleased; he'd always adored his uncle. In the beginning Zack had a part-time job, and he tried to contribute to the household by repainting the kitchen and retiling the downstairs bathroom. He and Joey laid new carpeting in Joey's room, cleared out the clogged gutters, and mended the loose lid on the washing-machine. He also wanted to wash the cars, but Basil put his foot down. That was the garden boy's job. Anyway, Zack repaired Joey's radio and my typewriter and swivel chair, and his own bicycle — many times. I used to imagine that when Brother Zack looked at a machine, the machine began to confide silently to him about how its inner self functioned and what ailed it. However, in the last year or so, he's grown very absent-minded, perhaps from too much meditating, and he doesn't seem as robust as he used to. But then we're all growing older, aren't we?

Now I have an uneasy feeling that something's wrong. When I came in, the house was silent, unusual for a Saturday afternoon. I was surprised to see Joey fast asleep on the couch, his face rather flushed, and when I tiptoed to Zack's room, I saw that he too had fallen asleep while sitting in that lotus position. And of course the girl was nowhere to be seen, probably jabbering away on some street corner. You know, these days …

I think I'll make myself some tea and maybe the noise from the kitchen will wake them both.

Uncle Zackie

Ag, I fell asleep and now Mom is in the kitchen. I wish I didn't have to move. My mouth tastes sticky and dry from the whiskey and I can smell how bitter my breath is. I shouldn't have had that third drink but I couldn't resist it after the way the second relaxed my shoulders and made my mind feel free. Then suddenly the alcohol came back to knock me out. I suppose because I'm very fit. They say the fitter you are the quicker you get shnookered.

I'll just slip out of the room and go check on Uncle Zackie before Mom does so.

Poor guy, he's fallen asleep, slipped over to one side, his knees still partly crossed. He's snoring so he must be a bit of okay. I'd better cover him with the quilt, and I'd better get outside to hide the crate and the rope before someone starts asking questions. I'm saying nothing to nobody if I can help it.

My In-Law

The man's a nut, but what can I do. The first time I met him I thought, hey, Ruth's got some funny relation. At our wedding reception he came up to me and said in that slow voice of his, 'Basil, so you really need sooo much food for these people?' I could only stare like a hooked fish at the guy, at those pale no-colour eyes and the fifties-style brush-cut. 'Sooo much,' he murmured, 'sooo much …' thinking

I suppose of the starving people in India or China or wherever.

One time when he was living in a back room of a house
on Sivewright we went to see him. At his one small window
opening onto the people's backyard, he had a grid on bricks
on which he'd laid out some slices of white bread.

'Why've you left the bread out there, Zack?' I asked.

'I'm making air toast, Basil,' he said.

'You're what?'

'Making air toast. You know, Basil, people waste a lot of
money on electricity these days. You'd never guess how
many watts one single piece of toast takes to make. And
we've got to conserve in this country. So I make my toast
without electricity. Out there the bread dries good and when
I bite it I get the *feel* of toast.'

'It's just plain old stale bread.'

'Don't say that!'

'Don't say what? Stale?'

'Yes, it's a word I don't like.' And he looked long-lipped,
his eyes pained. Then, what do you know, my kid, big-
hearted sap, comes forward and picks up a slice of bread
and bites into it. 'Mmmm ...' he says, 'nice. Has a real feel
of toast.' And he munches away.

When Zack first came to live with us he still had a three-
nights-a-week job as an aide in the men's ward at the Rand-
burg Clinic. It wasn't far from the house so he'd ride his
bike there and back. But then I found out that instead of
coming in through the back door in the early hours, he was
climbing up on the dustbin and letting himself into his room
through the window. I got the hell-in.

'For the lovamike, Zack, come in through the door, will
you!' I yelled.

'I don't want to be a bother, Basil.'

'You're not a bother, Zack! And I don't want you demon-
strating to burglars how to get into the house!'

'If you people are sleeping, I don't want to wake you,' he mumbled, rubbing his head just like some overgrown kid.

'You won't bladdy wake me!'

'Basil, please!' said Ruth.

'Well, he'll damnsure wake us if he falls out of the window,' I said, walking away, thinking what's the use.

So now what happens? I come home from golf and decide that before going in to change, I'll check on my new tomato and strawberry plants in the back garden, and what do I see? My kid Joey up on an apple-crate doing something with a rope over a branch of the blue gum.

'What're you doing up there, Joe?' I ask. 'Practice go so bad you want to hang yourself?' I'm joking of course.

Joey gives a sickly laugh. 'Oh, hello Dad,' he says. I look at him and see his face going pink down the sides. 'I was just a...a...' He jumps down trailing the piece of rope.

'What's the crate doing out of the shed?'

'Oh ... I ... ah ... I was standing on it, and ...'

'Yes, I saw you.'

Then Ruthie comes out looking worried.

'Joey, is Uncle Zackie not feeling good? I hope you didn't tire him out going shopping ...'

'We didn't go shopping, Mom.'

'Well, he's sleeping in an awkward position and his face is all pale and sweaty.'

'Something fishy's going on here,' I say. 'Listen to me, Joey, your mother and I want a straight answer. What were you doing with that rope and the crate? What's wrong with your uncle?'

'Dad, I was untying the rope.'

'For the lova ... I *know* you were untying it! I *saw* you!'

'Basil, no need to shout.'

'All right,' says the kid, sitting down on the crate and beginning to rub his head the way my In-Law does. 'You see,' he says in a fast breathy voice, 'Uncle Zackie tried to hang himself but I saw him in time and cut him down and ...'

'Oh my *God*,' says Ruth.

'Hang himself?' I ask.

'Yes,' says the kid. 'Something bad musta happened to him at the shops ...'

'Like *what?*' I am flabbergasted, I tell you.

'I dunno. I helped him inside and got him on his bed and asked him ... but he'll tell us later, he said.'

We all troop on inside and go to look at Zack. He's awake, staring up at the ceiling and talking softly to himself. He's got a bad-looking rope burn along one side of his chin. But do you think he'll tell us what got into him? Not on your life! He merely sits up, his pale eyes steady in his head, and says he made a mistake trying to kill himself and that death is not the path to take yet.

'Path?' I say, 'path?'

'Well, let's get you to a doctor, dear,' says Ruthie.

'No, Ruth, no,' says Zack.

'But you gotta treat that burn and have a check-up,' I say.

'Some salve and dressing'll do. Please ...' he says.

When Ruthie brings the stuff from the medicine cabinet, Joey insists on playing nurse, reminding us that he passed his First-Aid exam with distinction. Man, I wonder if my son's turning queer. Anyway, Ruth and I leave the two of them together, Joey gently spreading salve along Zack's chin and both of them now talking in low voices, something about an ice-pack and an arm-sling.

But I'm tired and I've had enough. I go get Zack's bicycle and put it in the shed, then I haul the crate and rope in too and lock the lot up. Zack is not traipsing around anymore on that bladdy bike. If he wants to go out, Ruthie or I'll take him, or Joey if it's somewhere close by. The man must act his age now. A bad feeling knits in my chest but I'm determined. I can't have any more scares from that old nutcase.

Zack

A common thief is a very low thing to be. I have never stolen anything in my life and I wouldn't do another person down by taking their property.

I'll never be able to walk proudly through True Value's again. Ag no, that is only the thought of today. Tomorrow I'll have a different thought. Tomorrow I'll go back and thank Frank Bezuidenhout properly for what he did for me. Besides I must get new screws for the crossbar of that bike of mine. If the rider trembles, that's all right, but the bike itself has to be steady. So says the Buddha. Oh-oh, that's sooo funny ...

THE WEDDING

'**S**tand *back* now,' said Mom to Dad.

Dad's forehead rippled angrily and his throat puffed full-blown, but he stepped back to stand next to his new wife, and Jessica in lowgear with gentle footfalls glided the few yards from the door to the desk, her path unimpeded by Dad's desire to be at her side. Her head was up, and the slithery white cloth, caught under her bosom with pink satin blossoms, slimmed her spacious hips.

Aaron took her arm lightly then released it self-consciously. They both stood in front of the magistrate standing behind Jessica's desk, which had been prepared for him with mindfulness and care. Here and there in the room were bowls of pink carnations flattered and escorted, as it were, by unglamorous white powdery plants. The magistrate wore no white Cinderella wig and academic gown, as Nita had childishly imagined that he would. Instead he had unbuttoned his suit jacket to present a cable-stitch cardigan, and as he lifted his head to clear his throat all present were allowed sufficient pause to gaze solemnly at his lustreless blackbrush moustache.

Dad turned his crumpled forehead and fat throat for sympathy to his new wife (please call me Germaine, she had said) but she shook her head at him slightly intimating *never mind dearest — what can one expect from these people*. Nita longed suddenly, to her own surprise, for some sign, some word (perhaps someone's real intensity of feeling would communicate itself), to transform them all into egoless celebrants, if only for ten minutes. After all, there was no use *now* in Mrs Goldberg, Aaron's mother, pretending to have a bad cold when everyone knew she had been crying, not only today but on and off for some weeks. She might have

59

put on a brave front and an orchid, as Mom and Germaine had done, even if she shunned a bloom like Mom's which rose ostentatiously to tickle her left ear.

Happy black Abednego was the last to step, humbly, with bending knees, into the room. He wore one of Billy's old suits pressed into sharp edges and spots of shimmer, and he held his hat in his hands as if it were a present for Jessica.

The magistrate started speaking to Jessica and Aaron. As they answered, in muted, shy voices, he filled in a form. Nita wondered what they thought of this meagre ritual. But then their choice of ceremonies had been limited for them. Aaron would not get married in a church; Jessica could not get married in the synagogue; and Mom's sense of what was right, her nerves in fact, would not permit them to be married in an ordinary shabby law-court. It was Barry who had suggested they get married in their own future flat. After all, what is a wedding, he had asked. You are simply being licensed. If you feel the necessity, you become licensed, then you become unlicensed, and, if you have either youth or energy, you become licensed again. Why make a fuss?

Jessica and Aaron were agreeing to something the magistrate had asked them, then they were signing some papers, and the proceedings were over or nearly over. The magistrate looked up at those who were present, then he stood up. He chose to gaze out of the window as he commenced giving Jessica and Aaron advice about the 'rocks', but Mrs Goldberg walked out of the room before he had finished speaking, and Nita found herself turning around to gaze after the woman's stiff back and thin red hair, teased and bouffant, resembling a delicate, unfinished bird's nest. She saw that Dad and Germaine, and Mom and Billy, her stepfather, had all turned to stare unhappily after Mrs Goldberg. The magistrate had also turned from the window to gaze after her. Nita felt sorry for him and strangely cast-down by the futility of, it seemed, life itself. She should pull herself together and try to leave the flat smiling. The bridal couple turned. Jessica had a fixed, wide-eyed smile on her face, but Aaron looked stern. He took his wife's elbow and pushed her along as if she could not find the doorway on her own. Barry, Nita's brother, roused her by pulling one of the bunched curls in her hair-do.

'Careful,' she said, 'You'll spoil my hair.'

'Christ! What a catastrophe *that* would be.'

His voice was acidic and Nita wondered whether, in spite of his attitude to licensing, he had expected something more.

On the pavement, a photographer, a cheaply-dressed little man with long, moist sideburns, started taking photos of them all. Nita felt foolish in her long pink dress and flow-ered headdress as she stood in the familiar street and saw passers-by and passengers in cars gape at them. She was glad to get into the bridal car and drive to the Goldberg's house for the reception.

People were already waiting for them there, as only the immediate family had been invited to the flat to see the marriage take place. The guests' cars were parked on both sides of the road and in the wide driveway and some on the lawn. In the dull sunset they crouched like shiny, sleepy beasts. *Jaguars*, particularly, always made Nita think of fast-creeping beasts.

The servants brought in trays of glasses of champagne, golden and discreetly effervescent, and the guests sipped carefully and talked quietly. Abednego had changed his jacket for a white coat and was also carrying a tray. He seemed so pleased with himself that Nita wondered whether Barry was still annoyed. He had been perversely cross when he heard that Abednego would be expected to carry a tray.

'Abednego should be a guest, an honoured guest,' he said to Mom. 'After all, he practically brought us up.'

'What exactly do you mean?' Mom had asked, and Billy had mumbled something about that effing Wits university.

'I am simply stating that Abednego should be a guest,' repeated Barry.

'Well, our family must also pull its weight,' Mom had said in a flat voice, not wishing to engage Barry in a further argument about the treatment of their old servant. As it was, Barry had added the subject of the wedding to the other sticky points which he constantly flung at their heads like so much adhesive confetti.

He had asserted that he would not wear a button-hole and that he would not make a speech. The whole idea filled him with nausea, he said. He wanted to know why he could not invite any of his Coloured friends and *why* Jessica was having an all-white reception. In this country, he shouted, any reception of any kind should inevitably be a multi-racial affair.

Jessica needed Barry to make a speech, as there was no one else who could do so. Billy, their stepfather, was a simply awful speaker. Simply awful, Jessica had moaned tearfully. Whereas Barry, who had degrees and was so clever and could speak so beautifully, was the very person to make a good impression. Eventually she said *she* didn't mind if Barry brought some of his Coloured friends and she went so far as to invite the two Indian women who were working on her wedding dress. So Barry agreed to make a speech, but warned the family that they should regret it. But they were all used to his warning them about things that could never happen. They were relieved.

Then Dad wrote from Natal that he wouldn't come to the wedding if he couldn't give Jessica away, but Mom said Billy should give her away, if anybody gave her away, because he had always paid all the accounts and was paying *this* one. The bickering was working on Mom's nerves, Nita could see, so she kept quiet when Jessica and Mom agreed that she should wear a stupid Regency-style satin dress in pink and have her hair gathered at the top of her head like a plump brown crowd of cocktail sausages. Then Jessica had a brain-wave. No one would give her away! Dad did come to the wedding, but he sulked.

Barry had also argued with Jessica over the dress. He asked her more than once whether she really intended going the whole medieval hog, sacrificial victim and all. Then Mom started mourning softly, but loud enough to be heard, that she wished Jessica had found a nice English or Afrikaans boy instead of causing complications. Finally, Billy, incensed, shouted that there were no more if onlies; marriage came suddenly. Then he walked away mumbling, 'like a big ...' He could be vulgar when he wanted to.

The reception room was now teeming with newly arrived guests who cluttered and chatted around the trays of drinks. Soft-pedalled platitudes and stiff wise smiles were disappearing. The talking and the laughing rose; even Jessica's wide glassy smile had relaxed into accustomed grooves. Everyone was speaking and no one was listening. Like a colony of frogs in a tepid pond, thought Nita. Only the two Indian women, dressed in lustrous saris, sat quietly together in a corner and sipped Fantas. Then the message was passed around that food was being served on the patio, which had been covered in blue and white striped canvas for the occasion. This prompted a well made-up woman with false eyelashes and a rusty, nicotined voice to ask Jessica: 'Do you know how to *feed* your man?'

'I'm learning,' said Jessica.

Nita heard with mild astonishment the assumed shyness and virginity in Jessica's voice. What a revelation her sister's new conjugal character was going to be for her! Suddenly Nita realized that Jessica had wanted a totally conventional wedding, and that she wanted to conform to the socially accepted patterns in life. Now Jessica was playing at being the bride in deadly earnest. That was why she tolerated the cloying sticky hand of the little girl who had, from the moment Jessica had stepped into the room, decided to cling to her. The child was hypnotized by the sight and rustle of the wedding dress, and hung onto Jessica, keeping in unison with her movements and stepping on her hem as her eyes gazed enchanted at the flowered headdress. And instead of disengaging herself, as Nita knew Jessica would normally have done, she constantly lowered her eyes madonna-like to the child's face.

Nita moved with the crowd down the passage to the patio. She became wedged between Dad and some aunt whom she barely recognized.

'Jessica is a brave girl to take on a horde like this!' said the aunt.

'You're right, by God,' said Dad. 'And they all look alike too — short, plump and over-fed. Well, I said what I thought about this wedding ... but no one would pay any attention to me, of course.'

'It's more noticeable, isn't it, because we ... I mean the Hamiltons are so tall. We're like ... thoroughbred racehorses compared to ... to ...'

'Pigs!' said Dad.

Nita bent her head to one side so that the woman's hot breath could not explode against her exposed neck, and she tried to wriggle past Dad in order to escape the cushiony breasts pressing against her back. But her path was blocked on all sides.

'Do I congratulate you, Uncle Rick?' asked a cousin who had pushed her way up to Dad.

'You do *not!*'

'That's not worthy of you, dear,' said Dad's new wife. 'Please excuse him,' she said to the cousin. 'He's upset. This poor man has suffered *so!*'

'Yes,' he said. 'But my sufferings started a long time ago. Thirty years, to be exact, when I married that *woman*.'

'Well, never mind that now,' said the aunt.

'But she has pushed this wedding. I'm telling you. She was always mad about money, and you can see by this that the Goldbergs have money. To encourage *my* daughter to marry a Jew ... and you'll notice that Aaron hasn't been near me yet! Oh, the breeding shows ... the breeding shows!'

Dad stopped speaking. His face was red and his throat quivered. Nita said loudly, 'Do excuse me,' and forced her way through the crowd. She heard Dad's new wife asking with slow reasonableness in her voice, 'Surely the *real* father of the bride should give her away?'

The guests were swaying and nudging and leaning and excusing themselves around the tables. They seemed to be desperate with hunger. Forks, three at a time, were dug into the smoked salmon so that large thick portions were pulled this way and that because nobody would let them go. Cheese soufflé was being slopped and hammered onto the plates with over-large spoons, and the general problem seemed how to put enough unpeeled crayfish onto a plate and still retain space for other delicacies. Nita had never been able to manage a plate and fork while standing up, so she made a half-hearted attempt to eat with her fingers without casting decorum to the winds. But her appetite was small, so she contrived to find an empty surface on which to place her half-filled plate.

Before the dessert was laid out, Mr Goldberg called for silence and the guests composed themselves for the speeches. When Barry was called on, Nita's perturbation which had begun at breakfast increased to the point where she contemplated escape. She looked toward the door, but that was entirely barricaded with bodies, whispering, tittering and lifting champagne glasses. She turned to face her brother.

'Ladies ... and ... gentlemen ...' he began in excellent accent. He was the only person Nita knew who had benefited from private speech lessons.

'... my sister asked me to speak at her wedding, and ... I agreed ... chiefly because, well ... this wedding being the uniting of two ... er ... groups ... I ... er ... saw it as, well, symbolic of a ... situation much to be desired in this country.'

The guests had not been completely quiet when Barry started speaking, but at this point there was dead silence except for the faint dull sounds of dishes clattering and the nattering of African women which came from the kitchen. There were several exchanges of quizzical glances and slight *moues*. Jessica and Aaron, standing on Barry's right, both looked solemnly at the wall above the guests' heads.

'There are too many groups in this country,' continued Barry more firmly. 'And too many attempts to exaggerate their differences. I advocate ... a ... constructive unity and ... er ... co-operation between all the groups ... in this country, irrespective of their divergent ... er ... different colours, creeds and ... er ... social positions!'

Some of the male guests were looking with scientific detachment into their glasses. Nita wondered whether they were attempting to break communication with the speaker by not looking at him. Perhaps they were simply bored.

'Now ... a wedding such as this is ... well ... symbolic. Both parties are prepared to share their different ... cultures ... and to be tolerant of ... divergent ... divergent ... convictions.'

Barry paused and consulted the slip of paper in his hands. A restless ripple moved through the people standing before him at the other side of the table. Nita saw that Barry was not happy, was not in his element as she had expected he would be. He had long shadows under his eyes, though they could have been signs of an old hangover from the night before.

'When I meet a person, I try to find out what he is *doing* about the situation we all *know* exists here.'

Barry seemed to have made up his mind to reach his conclusion. He spoke fast, almost harshly.

'We whites enjoy a privileged position. Many people are suffering to enable us to enjoy this position. What are we doing to try to even out the imbalance? We all have a debt … a vast debt … to pay. I cannot accept a person as a friend unless I know … that he is … at least aware that he owes this … debt. Jessica and Aaron are aware of their debt. They have declared their intention of settling it … as far as possible … and I see their wedding as a strengthening … the one with … er … by … the other to … settle this debt. They can work *together* to do their … their bit. So … I ask you to raise your glasses with me to … drink to this … this union in strength.'

The guests drank. Someone started singing for they are jolly good fellows, and other voices joined in, but the singing was thin. Then Aaron stepped forward and briefly thanked everyone and wished them an enjoyable evening. Nita felt morbidly sorry for her whole family, and wondered whether it was the champagne. She pitied Barry in his present intense self-consciousness. She pitied Jessica in her failure to obtain an entirely conventional wedding. Barry had said no words of praise for Jessica and Aaron, as was usual at weddings, and Jessica must have realized that the guests were disappointed in not being regaled with the expected humour, extravagance and tactful salaciousness in the wedding speeches. She pitied her mother and Billy who were losing touch with their children and would never achieve 'touch' with the Goldberg family. And she pitied Dad his bitterness.

Dessert was served, and soon after guests started leaving. Nita decided to search for aspirin in the kitchen to ease the soft hammering in her right temple. She put her head round the kitchen door. The noise was tremendous. There were four or five African women washing and drying dishes and packing them away. Towers and towers of dishes stood on the sink and on the kitchen table. They were all talking and laughing stridently. Abednego was there too, busy pouring little bits of booze from nearly-empty glasses into an enamel mug. Nita drew her head back and went through to the front lounge. Mom and Billy were sitting together tiredly, both looking middle-aged and rumpled. Mom's pearls had shifted tipsily around so that the sparkling diamante clasp was twinkling at the side of her neck. Her orchid had unhealthy brown flecks on its enamel-looking leaves. They were waiting for Abednego.

Nita drove home with Barry who had managed to get fairly drunk in a short space of time.

'Dad made me so bloody cross!' he said.

'Never mind that now, Barry,' said Nita.

'He's never realized that fatherhood is more than just a good bang ...'

'Barry!' said Nita.

'He never put his hand in his pocket toward this wedding, but he sulked the whole bloody time because he wasn't in the limelight.'

'Never mind, man.'

'Oh, I get so mad ... so mad ... names and tags ... put people into pigeonholes ... Jesus I get so mad! Yah, you're a yid and you're a goy, and you're a ... a ... dago, and you're a goddam coolee, and you're a kaffir, and you're a ... a ...' He paddled his left hand up and down excitedly.

'Barry, watch the road, man,' said Nita.

CARLOTTA'S VINYL SKIN

My friend David, a successful lawyer who helped me with my immigration papers for this country, is unhappy in a niggled, half-tortured sort of way because of the unimpressive salary I earn as an English professor. Once a month regularly he will phone me to beg me to write a lurid romantic novel that might get on the best-seller list and enable me to buy the house and car he thinks I owe it to myself to own. I have told him over and over again that I *cannot* write such a novel — I would become immobilized with ennui and self-disgust at my very typewriter. I would waste my time trying, and simply be inserting my hands and head into a stock-like writer's block.

'Sheila, can't you just prostitute yourself for *once?*' he pleads. 'Just once. Then you could keep writing the egghead stuff no one wants to read in comfort, at least.'

Sometimes a little inner voice joins its harangue with his. *If* I have endurance and energy (which perhaps I don't have and am therefore lacking the essentials of a full human being) I could indeed write a money-bringing book, the voice insists. Think up a simple plot, set it in a foreign country during a time of turmoil. Be prepared to write six hundred pages. Create a beautiful heroine who falls in love with a rebel/renegade/revolutionary/freedom fighter/innocent fugitive from justice/political activist/disinherited son later to be re-inherited/wildcat unionist/or even a handsome Dracula-like fellow, eyes heavy-lidded, soul possessed. Or she could be in search of a lost father. Contrive to have the lovers separated and then bring them together in a grand finale. They are both, or all three, hot-blooded. Here's your chance, Sheila, to portray the sex act from the woman's point of view. You could do a service to womankind while making money.

Weaving, weaving, I stick a sheet of paper in the typewriter. A foreign country? The only country I know well, whose landscape forms part of my own mental baggage, is South Africa. My setting will have to be South African — it's foreign enough to most Americans and it's their money I'm after. I couldn't presume to write about America: I know too little about American turmoil and even less about the various historic sites. I have no doubt that I could recreate in words the look of the Cape coast, the Karroo, the Bushveld, the Highveld, the Natal highlands, the Drakensberg. In fact, if I invented a country, calling it something like Sylvanvakia or Prinsenmania or Eendt-sur-Mer, I would only end up describing either the Cape coast, the Karroo, the Bushveld, the Highveld, the Natal highlands, or the Drakensberg. Geography is destiny.

Turmoil? If I want this book to sell, I have to keep all racial discrimination or conflict out of it, except for a bit of jungle-enshrouded sex to the beat of tom-toms, but that could come into the sub-plot. So I could go along with the myth of the 'white man's' war and set my story in South Africa on the eve of Anglo-Boer hostilities. My heroine will be a peaches-and-cream English girl who comes out with her wealthy father to visit the mines and falls in love with ... an Afrikaner? No, no. A descendant of the 1820 Settlers? A South African English Gentleman and a Rebel. How about that?

I visualize delicate Victorian blouses, thick blonde hair done up in a chignon, large hats, many petticoats, soft white hands, large blue eyes, a vulnerable but brave mouth. Oh no, I am regurgitating memories of Bo Derek starring in *Tarzan the Ape Man*. Why does schlock always stick? I must start afresh. I *must* start afresh. The image of one of my best-looking writing students comes to mind. She has slightly curly, untidy brown hair, a thin face, and slanting catlike eyes. She usually wears long peasant skirts or calf-length tight trousers in Hot Pink or Luminous Blue, and soft suede boots with a foldover at the ankle, such as medieval pages must have worn, three ear-rings in one ear and none in the other, oversized T-shirts or fifties blouses. I try dressing her in a Victorian outfit. She looks okay although her shoulders are a bit broad and she stands rather sardonically and firmly on the ground surveying the desolation of a burnt-down Free State farm. Allie, get those boots off, and for God's sake, wilt a little!

Get her off that farm. I'll send her in a donkey cart with her wealthy but dying father into the interior. They are on their way to Kimberley. But the father dies on the road and she is left a pile of money. I love bumping off fathers in my stories; like other egghead writers, I am haunted by Oedipus, Electra, and Jocasta.

So there she is alone, on her way to Kimberley. She will have to have picked up some passengers, though. Poor girl. Look, I'm sorry, but I have to think about these things: how will she wash properly on the road? Wonderful complexions don't stay that way without cleansing. How will she be able to urinate and move her bowels out in the bush with all those skirts on? Just bundle them up? But won't they still get splashed and stained? How much toilet paper does her party have? Did they *have* toilet paper in those days? Did they have toothbrushes? When was the first toothbrush marketed, hey you Popular Culturists? What if she gets her period? Of *course* she'll get her period, unless she's anorexic. But an anorexic girl won't be able to handle the boisterous sex scenes in the book. And what about mosquitoes? I mean, have you *ever* spent a night out of doors in the summer without netting and that new insecticide you rub on hands, face, and feet, or whatever parts of the body are exposed? The perspiration! The food going bad!

Let me tell you, I know from experience that when my skin breaks out, I lose all sense of the romantic occasion. I don't feel like going to bed with some guy whose skin is fine and who'll want to leave the light on while we make love. I don't like making love when I'm sweaty or dirty. I don't fancy sweaty or dirty men. Also, I find it excruciating to be 'confined' with a man in bed, or even in a car, when I'm suffering from flatulence. Yes, contrary to masculine belief, women *do* fart. Over the centuries we've worked hard to establish the conviction of our continence. But out in the bush the pretence would have to go. I simply cannot muster up enthusiasm for Romance as I regard Carlotta, my beautiful heroine, waddling like a duck as she squats, searching for a place to hold steady where the tough grass won't prick her bare butt.

In my imagination my student Allie walks into my office. Today she is sporting an old stained braided coat of the kind major-domos of hotels wear, a limp mini skirt and army boots. I know that she (like many other students these days) buys her clothes from a popular second-hand clothing store that sometimes stocks astonishing antique garments, things people have stolen out of their grandparents' attics, or defunct theatre companies have hawked. Allie has on bottle-green tights and a little head-hugging hat from the twenties.

'Why do you want to write that trash?' she asks me.

'To make money.'

'Then you've got to stop thinking about physical discomfort. Your heroine has to have skin of vinyl, teeth of white stainless steel (if that is possible), her polyfibrous hair does not grow damp and scraggly, and her crystalline eyes have the three or four necessary expressions, depending on the light, for your purposes: joy, indignation, love, and sorrow. She doesn't have periods, or perspiration, or pee, or poo!'

'I can't write about a vinyl *dummy*,' I say, my own eyes flashing indignantly.

'What is the least you can write about?'

'Well, to begin with, I need to see real people in my

mind's eye, a woman like you, for instance. Say, what does your boyfriend do?' Deep down in me a little hope is born that she will say he is completing training as an officer in the Air Force Academy. A shadowy Richard Gere starts forming. *Would* such a gorgeous thing date Allie the Punk in her tights and boots?

'My boyfriend has a degree in Agriculture, but because of the recession he can't find a job in his field, no pun, so he's working as a male nurse at Hannah Hospital. Oh boy, you wouldn't believe the kinds of things he's learned to do! Give people enemas, stick catheters into them, give them shots in the bee-hind, and hold pans for them when they want to throw up. But it's done him good, especially seeing old people naked and having to wash the shit off them and all that. He's much more sympathetic toward people these days. He never criticizes women for their bodies the way most guys do.'

'What does he look like?' I ask, a bit disconsolately, pulling the paper out of the machine.

'He's no Mister Universe. He's okay. He's going to have to go on a bit of a diet because of the tummy he's getting. Twenty-five's too young to get a tummy. Not that I mind. He's got a sweet face, but his skin is very pale. He can't suntan at all: he just goes red, mostly his nose, and he was never good at sports at school because of his flat feet. Would you listen to this: no one realized that he was flat-footed until he was about fourteen? He got out of the swimming pool at school and by chance the coach noticed his wet footprint. As flat as a fish.'

'What will he do? Keep looking for a job in his "field" or settle for nursing?'

'Naa ... he's decided to go on to grad school next year. He may as well. He's saved enough to put himself through, and he still wants to get into some branch of agricultural science, maybe at a higher level.'

'And you?'

'I'll keep on with my studio art. Though I wouldn't mind farming. I've always wanted to farm. That's why Percy and I get on so well.' She settles herself on the corner of my desk, running one hand over a pile of books. I see that each fingernail is painted a different colour. She looks at me confidentially. 'You know, Percy my boyfriend had a terrible time as a kid. His mom used to dominate him totally. Even when he was in high school she'd clean his room and go through all his things. She'd even examine the underclothes he'd thrown in the wash. He had no privacy whatsoever. And the one time he came home a little drunk, both his parents created such a scene, even though he was already twenty-one, that now he simply can't, *he can't* drink in front of them. Now his dad offers him beers and beers and beers, but he can't accept them. I've had a lot of trouble getting him to loosen up with me, you know. Do you know he stayed a virgin until he was twenty-four?'

'Allie, you don't have to tell me all this stuff.'

'I know you'll keep it to yourself.'

'Of course.'

'I had to teach him a lot,' she says coolly, getting off the desk and clumping to the door, her boots heavy against the floorboards. 'I hope you can write your Romance and make some big bucks,' she adds, but without much interest. She wiggles her painted nails at me and leaves. I put the paper back into the typewriter.

My story begins to take form. Percy, my male protagonist (I dare not call him a hero, which is not to say he isn't heroic) will be a civilian helper in the military hospital at Bloemfontein where more British soldiers are dying of diarrhoea than are being killed by the Boers. But I won't go into details that will nauseate the reader. I might draw a Daumieresque picture of grey skeletal bodies with sombre young faces in overcrowded wards. But Percy is a short, shy, pink-faced-fellow with not too noticeably flat feet and a deep desire to be a farmer. He has never known a woman (in the biblical sense) until he meets Petronella, a farm girl who has had to take on many of the chores at 'Bloustroom' because the men are away fighting in the Transvaal. She wears army boots and hitches up her skirts for ease of movement by means of an old cartridge belt. She ties her hair up in pony tails with string, which causes her cotton sunbonnet to sit oddly on her head. The neighbours think she is eccentric if not mad (The Mad Woman of Africa — cliché alert!) and no young man comes riding up to 'Bloustroom' to court her when the farmer-fighters are on leave. But Percy doesn't notice anything out of the ordinary about Petronella. Besides, he is lonely. His widowed mother, who wielded inflexible control over his life, has herself passed on to the Fathers as a result of a stray shell crashing through Percy's suburban bedroom just as she was about to riffle through the things her son stores in his tin trunk. (Am I killing Mothers off too now?)

Petronella has great trouble with stomach wind, mostly because of the high-starch diet forced on all the population, but Percy is unaware of her sneaky farts — because of his job, his hair and clothes are infused with excremental and medicinal smells. One afternoon in the barn, she shows him how to make love (*this* will be my main sexual scene, putting male readers straight about female arousal once and for all), whereafter he becomes insatiably attracted to her. He nearly gets shot by the British at one point because they suspect that he is consorting with the enemy, but Petronella is not the enemy nor do any of the enemy come near her. But Percy goes to jail (SAD scene), and the British burn Petronella's farm (TRAGIC scene, Petronella's unusual silhouette seen against the brilliant orange and blues of the fire). But after the war Percy marries Petronella and takes up farming with her — her father and brother died in prison camps set up by the British for Boer prisoners in the West Indies. This information is conveyed to Petronella in a letter written by General de Wet, a letter which she frames.

My telephone rings. 'Sheila, honey …' (it is David, my lawyer-friend), 'I've just been reading in the Free Press about a housewife in Troy, Michigan, I mean *Troy*, Michigan! And she's making plenty of money writing these novels to a formula. Apparently her publishers supply her with an outline which she merely fleshes out. Now you could do that!'

The strong picture I have of Petronella and Percy clearing away the debris of the burnt-down farm house begins to dissipate. Behind them I see beautiful Carlotta, her blonde hair wisping the sides of her lovely vinyl skin, her lacy petticoats caught up against the breeze in one small hand, her lips pursed redly in anticipation. She waves. At a handsome horseman? No, at me. I am surprised. I see that she wants me to bring her to life, rescue her from that vinyl skin, allow her to experience hot tearful afternoons of toothache, days when she can't get a comb through her sweating hair, the bloated feeling of food moving through her digestive system, messy periods at the wrong time, just when she wanted to wear a white gown to the officers' dinner, and she wants me to give her the good sense to guide her lover's hand and penis so that they move in ways she wants, instead of having to submit to one of those writhing, grunting, quick, harsh sex acts always inflicted on Romantic heroines. I hesitate. I do pity her. Mmm … Carlotta could be Petronella's cousin from overseas. Percy introduces her to Captain Coninghame, the Chief Surgeon. Carlotta uses part of her fortune to rebuild Petronella's farm.

'Look, David, I don't think I want some publisher's outline. I can think up my own outline,' I say.

'Don't tell me I've persuaded you to *do* it?'

'I am thinking about … the project … very seriously.'

'I mean, if someone in Troy, Michigan, can do it, so can you.'

'Ja, ja, I'm thinking about it,' I say, beckoning to Carlotta.

TO LEAVE THIS PLACE

I thought, how will I bear to leave this place again after this? How will I stand the deprivation to my senses? Here, with Barend smelling of honey-suckle shaving lotion and nicotine, his tongue licking at the longer hairs growing at the sides of his moustache, and my ribs tightening as I think of lying in bed with him. The pliant Mercedes blowing in just the right amount of heat, its fine works whispering. So smooth. All my life I have owned small cheap cars, soon developing rattles and troubles. What comfort now, I thought, for these two days, to drive in luxury, with the resplendent spread of sky like a silk sail and veld undulating yellow and black. There were lines of leafless papery willows in hollows where stream-beds must have lain. All this is mind-obliterating, I thought. Too beautiful. The colors ran through me and I asked myself, was it always this beautiful? Have I forgotten so much in the years I have been away? I did not want to move a muscle. Immobile, I wanted to gape. You know, the clarity of light was so stark I felt I could taste the smoke coming from passing clusters of huts, and crunch the familiar bitterness of scorched grass under foot. I realize now it was impossible to smell or hear or taste what is outside a speeding airtight Mercedes.

After a while the car and my mood gave me the weight-less sensation I imagined those two birds knew as they hung motionless in the air before gliding to disappear behind red and brown chiselled rock outcrops surrounded by girdles of thorn trees. When Barend said, 'Stacey, my girl ...' I turned my head with reluctance at first and then with a sweet taste in my mouth at the sight of him. He was very at ease, steering the car with only three fingers of his right hand while the left arm lay along the seat behind my back. He smiled. He has even teeth. The silver strands of his hair and beard caught the light. He was like a godling, a middle-aged godling. I was his 'old girlfriend', in his words, but I was no goddess now. I thought, this Mercedes is like a chariot for us; a womblike chariot. How pleasant.

'Stacey, there's beer in the cooler on the back seat. Pull one out for me please. Have one yourself.'

We drank and the world went by purring. Birds in vee-formation swooped and wove through the air, and very few cars came from the opposite direction to distract us. We drove and drank and talked desultorily. Then we were silent, and I began waiting for the sun to set, as it does only in Africa, waiting for the brilliant blood curtain to come down. I grew tense with anticipated pleasure.

'It'll be dark before we get there. I hope I don't miss the turn-off,' said Barend, grinning at me. His mouth is wide so his smiles are never tight. I love your mouth, I wanted to say, and your smell, and your car, and this landscape you are driving me by, through, across. I want to do this forever and ever, transfixed in time, drunk with beer and beauty. But I said, 'Please don't miss the turn-off.'

It being mid-winter there was virtually no dusk. Within the hour the sun had spun rapidly behind us, sending embers to comet across the blue, splashing redly the occasional oncoming car, and staining in peaceful pink the eastern horizon toward which we were headed. Lovely, lovely, I thought, turning in my seat to look at the splendid burning ball behind us. I thought, this landscape has become wondrously strange and yet platitudinous to me: it comes to me as if I am watching a technically superb movie of Africa. Later that thought would bother me but then I was too happy.

'Is it pretty?' asked Barend, looking in his rearview mirror.

'Yes, magnificently pretty …'

I thought, one day I would like to make love in a comfortable car like this, sitting astride the man, coming and coming as the sun expands and explodes like this, holding the moment, as if putting my senses on cruise-control. I looked at Barend, remembering the back seat of his old Volkswagen. He winked at me with both eyes as if he too were thinking, *later*.

Then it was over and the shadows disappeared and everything flattened and began greying.

'Another beer?' I asked Barend as I rooted among the loosening melted ice in the cooler, trying to keep out of my voice any semi-quaver of disappointment.

'Yes, please,' he said.

It grew dark. I could feel my stomach beginning to cramp slightly with hunger. The beer seemed to have created a hollow windy emptiness in me. I thought, I hate the way one always has to pay a price even for the mildest heightened sensation and reckless urge whether induced by alcohol or not. 'Will there be food ... dinner, Barend?' I asked.

'No, you are going to have to starve,' he joked. 'That's my ploy, you see. I take women out to the farm and starve them so that they are too weak to resist me.'

'I am already weak,' I said. I could have added, In too many ways.

'Don't worry. Heinie and his girl should be there already, building the fire. When we arrive the coals will be just right for the steaks,' he said.

'Explain to me again who are Heinie and Hidemi. I know he's your partner at the law firm ...'

'Ja. And we play golf together and drink. We both like taking our women friends out to the game-farm on weekends. Heinie's been seeing Hidemi for some time. I think he's kind of infatuated with her. But, obviously, he doesn't want to harm his marriage.'

'Oh ...' I thought, maybe Barend's seeing me could harm *his* marriage. But I decided not, having heard that he had other more recent and probably more regular women friends.

He did miss the right turn-off. The car hummed us into a moonless darkness between uneven black walls of dense bush, and headlights forming a lit sandy pool moving ahead of us, and the tiny square light from the turned-on radio glowing on our noses as we bent forward, peering. The bell-like throatiness of someone singing a love song was threatening to stupefy me with vague disappointed longings when Barend slowed down and made a gravelly u-turn. We headed back to a village we had passed earlier and stopped at a gas-station for directions. Both attendants knew where Van Wyk's game-farm was, and we sped out of the town's lights into the darkness again.

'There are the gates,' said Barend with a relieved explosion of breath, guiding the car into a short driveway in front of large locked iron gates. From a thatched cubicle to one side an old stooped African emerged, carrying what looked like a ledger. When Barend lowered his window to take the book and sign us in, the cold air flowed over us, bringing a smell of blue gums and blackjacks and sand, and a thin smokiness. The tones of Barend and the old man's voices were lowered as they spoke to each other in Afrikaans; the soothing sounds of human friendliness. 'Baie dankie, ou Vader,' said Barend. Old Father. 'Goeie nag.' Good-night. Good-night old Father. I put my hand on Barend's knee, liking him so much, feeling the flow of bones and sinews as his foot pressed a pedal. With the care of a mother wheeling a sleeping child in a pram, he edged the car over a rutted path that jostled our shoulders together companionably, round through the edging of thorn trees, until the road opened out and the farmhouse came into sight. It was an L-shaped structure, also thatched. In the backyard a campfire burned and moving human figures threw huge shadows.

'Who lives here?' I asked softly.

'All year round? No one,' he said in a normal voice. 'The owner comes sometimes on a weekend or for summer vacations. He lets his friends use the place when he's not here, people like Heinie and me.'

'So it's only us and ...'

'Heinie and Hidemi. You'll meet them now.'

We parked and walked across the stones to the paved yard while the two figures, flickering black and red in the firelight, waited for us. The man seemed enormous but the woman, in contrast, ephemeral. As he stepped forward she was engulfed in his shadow, but then reappeared, the light touching a pale oriental face surrounded by thick black hair. Their eyes were cavernous and I suppose ours were too. The smell of broiling meat brought a rush of saliva to my mouth.

'Hey guys, this is Stacey from the United States,' said Barend. 'Or maybe I should call you *Statesy*,' he laughed, his hand firm on the back of my neck, pushing me forward. 'I met this girl at a demonstration on the Cape Town campus, God, it must be fifteen years ago ...' He kissed me lightly on the temple. 'So we've known each other a long time now. But she deserted us five years ago. Isn't that disgusting? This is her first visit home ...' Heinie and Hidemi were offering their hands. 'I decided I had to help her remember how nice this country is, so I brought her out here ...' Barend laughed again, no irony in his voice.

The greetings of the others were muted. Careful, I thought. They would want to know whom they were dealing with before they relaxed with me. I was one of those who had taken the 'chicken run', I realized. To their minds I could be one of those who, safe in America, pickets in the streets or trespasses South African embassies, knowing there will be no repercussions. Perhaps I pretend to American friends to be wanted by the South African Security Police. I saw them picturing me sitting in an air-conditioned living-room, cocktail in hand, jeering at a television picture of police in a township, I having lost in the abundance of entertainment all sense of this world itself and its uncontrollable fragmenting like the floor of a dried-up dam. I pose as dissident, refugee, critic. I make myself look good. Professional South African.

'What a beautiful night,' I said going closer to the fire and rubbing my hands together. 'Mmm … smells wonderful …'

'These are my hors d'oeuvres,' said Heinie, poking with a fork at king prawns the size of one of his own fleshy fingers, at segments of sausage and medallions of fillet ready at the edge of the grill. 'Then comes the main course,' he explained, turning his head to a platter of steaks. 'I have made the *sarad*,' said Hidemi in a low accented voice, handing us glasses. Her actions were delicate but wide, like a dancer learning steps, and I could smell her rosewater fragrance over the odour of cooking food. Heinie poured the wine for us, though his eyes like mine were on Hidemi. I wished the light were brighter so that I could see her better. She seemed terribly young. All evening Heinie touched her, petted her, pulled her to him at every opportunity. He was like a boy with a new much-loved animal that would not stay put.

We sat in garden chairs around the fire, eating and drinking. We all spoke in low voices as if speaking loudly or even normally would be an offence against the dense evenness of the night, against the almost inaudible thrumming presences in the trees and the rustling of living creatures among the shadows: an offence even against the stars that hung fatly overhead just out of arm's reach. At times there were the far-off snapping of twigs, unidentifiable calling noises, and short harsh feral coughs. Jakkals, said Barend. Then he spoke about the recent car-bombings. After a silence Hidemi telling sadly and haltingly a story of how on Okinawa Island in her mother's day, all the young girls and women were handed small bombs and grenades and instructed to blow themselves up if they were approached by the landing GIs. All women were to die with honour rather than be raped, and many did blow themselves up, quite needlessly, it transpired. The GIs were particularly well-behaved.

'How awful,' I said.

'That won't happen to our women here. They'll have guns in their hands,' said Heinie angrily. Then he changed the subject. He spoke at length about his new Honda Helix, then about wind-surfing, and the devaluation of the rand currency. But the matter of money set Barend talking about strikes, riots, and the role of the trade unions. Ultimately we all agreed sombrely, our voices old seventy-eight records rotating and rotating, that the whole system had to change.

When the fire started sinking Barend got up and went to fetch us each a blanket from the house, and we sat hunched, mostly silent, warmly covered up, Heinie digging morosely at the embers with a stick and Hidemi gazing upwards, head thrown back, as if in a trance. I thought, we are all thought-ful; we are heartsore. It is the fire crumbling away and the darkness and our being so out of time, sitting in the dry win-ter night air as if we were earth's earliest dwellers, whereas we know we have already lost all this — if we ever rightfully owned it. We are melancholy: we are like tired children who have played too long. At last Heinie said, 'It's time for bed. Come, my girl …' He took Hidemi's hand.

Our bedroom was achingly cold. The air was like dry ice to my nostrils and I coughed.

'I'm sorry, but there's no central heating out here, you know,' said Barend. He laughed, coughing too, and patting me on the shoulder. Shivering I hastily undressed and pulled on a sweatsuit to sleep in. We took it in turns to use the small even icier bathroom, then climbed between the taut clammy sheets of the bed. We lay facing each other, hugging and blowing noisily into the bed to help warm ourselves. I could feel Barend's moustache prickling my nose, and under the flannel pyjamas he wore he felt to my hands as I remembered him. Then he wrapped one leg round both of mine and smothered me to his chest. More hair curling over the top button of the pyjamas tickled my face. His beard, like my hair, smelled of woodsmoke and meat and cigarettes. It grew warmer. We started pecking, then kissing with slower preoccupation. I thought, what can be more wonderful than this day, this evening, this night, on this momentarily quiet earth with no moon, no sound, no wind, no trouble. Old sadness like new fears were like plankton washed up on a beach, now floated back out to sea on the tide of warmth that whooshed in my ears. Our teeth touched. We nicked each other's lips and tongues. We were barracuda bobcats chaffinches snakes. His moving hands changed my breasts into pigeons fluttering, beaks open. He wet my face with his saliva and dried it with his breath.

After a while it seemed that we were struggling together like inept teenagers. I relaxed and tried to draw a normal breath.

'Old friend, my dear old friend,' said Barend hoarsely in my ear. 'I don't know …' But he was pulling at my sweatpants, dragging them to my knees, and then hooking them off my feet with his toes.

'What? What's the matter?' The room's air slipped coldly between us.

'I don't know what's wrong with me. But I can't seem to manage …'

'Shall we go and crawl into the back seat of the Mercedes and pretend it's the Volkswagen?' I said, partly to hide my disappointment and partly hoping that this remembrance of our former love-making might rouse him.

'I don't think that will help,' he said flatly.

'Then let's leave it,' I said, bending to reach for my pants.

'No, no, keep still.' Barend's hands on my shoulders were like a physician's. 'Keep still,' he repeated.

'But if you don't feel like it, then I don't.'

'It's not that I don't feel like it. God knows that I do. I just can't seem to do it. Ag ... perhaps I have known you too long, you know. And then you left ...'

'Well, no matter. Let's sleep.' My eyes used to the dark could see the feathery edges of his grey hair against the pale wall and the lustre of one eye as he raised himself on an elbow.

'I'll take care of you,' he said, one hand on my thigh.

'No, let's just sleep.'

'No, no, I won't hear of it.'

'Yes, yes,' I insisted.

In the morning at the breakfast table in the farmhouse kitchen, I could see Heinie and Hidemi more clearly. He was a tall freckled Afrikaner with nicely combed strawy straight hair, heavy legs, and strong sloping shoulders. Like Barend he had been a rugby player in university and was now a successful lawyer.

In that early light Hidemi's skin was as flat and pallid as unstirred cream, and her black eyes suggestively inexpressive, allowing one to interpret nuances for oneself. She would not let me help her, but alone served us bacon and eggs, her gestures large graceful angular. Her mouth was a short straight line, lipless and childish. It was her hair that formed a contrast to her pallor and containment. It was very long and she had had it permed so that it fanned out about her head, light, black, electric. Her clothes were elegantly loose and layered, tied with several scarves. It was clear to me why Heinie found her stunning. And then I wondered what Heinie's wife was like and what Barend's wife was like. I wondered whether both their wives remained as unchanging and as knowable as I had to Barend. Yet, Barend had not changed for me, while his sameness remained attractive. Suddenly, however, my eyes on Hidemi's long thin supple fingers, I understood Heinie's greed for the other, the outsider, and for an instant I was jealous.

Afterwards the two Mercedes went off in different directions. Heinie was to drop Hidemi off in Pretoria, while Barend was determined that I should see what wildlife there was on the farm. He let the car crawl and lumber over narrow paths, and we saw giraffe, dappled swanlike ungainly, against gnarled branches and blue sky, and some deer with flickering ears. 'Look there,' Barend hissed, pointing to three baboon sitting on a rock as if posing for a family photograph. 'There is a leopard somewhere...' he murmured. 'I'm sure there is a leopard.'

But the sun was too high and bright, drawing off what colour there was from the arid surfaces. The long grass was bleached, the sand burnt to pale russet, and the trees looked as if they would never again absorb moisture. I could not bring myself to say, let's go. Barend kept manoeuvring the car to find for me some astounding animal, some sight to stir me, some memory to take back to the States. To compensate me, perhaps? To keep me here? No, that I could not believe.

'Look there,' he said. 'That's an iguana. You must never take it for some sort of lizard. And keep your eyes on the branches. I know there are some young mambas ...'

'Why do you want me to see snakes? I don't like snakes,' I said, my voice light with pretended amusement.

'I want you to see everything.'

'Why?'

'Because you may not get another chance.'

'Why not?'

'Why not? Good God, look what's happening to this country ... Oh well, let's go home.' He accelerated slightly and took a path heading in the direction of the big gates.

'Ach, what's the use ...' he said, almost to himself. I could not bring myself to say, But Barend, it's been wonderful. I sat in a kind of dumb blinded blankness.

On the road back to the village we passed several cars filled with families wearing church clothes. Sometimes we could see the slender shape of a rifle stacked next to the driver. I was sure each car had a handgun in the glove compartment, as did Barend's Mercedes.

Barend insisted on stopping in the town to buy the Sunday newspapers. He handed the thick pile to me as he got back in the car, but the headlines being so frightful, I threw the papers on the back seat, not prepared to attend to them yet. I thought, feeling a thin sense of loss, Barend has given up on our friendship. But I said nothing. What was there to say?

All the way home I watched the bleak stubbly veld closely, though, hoping I would spot some object or plant or bird, something unusual, so that I could say to Barend, look there, look there, oh Lord, wasn't that wonderful? But the midday sun eventually forced us to put on dark glasses and him to put his foot down. Silent, concentrating, we sped back to Johannesburg.

CARRIED AWAY BY THE MOMENT

This story is about Uwe Wenzel. Perhaps you met him or even got to know him at the meetings on Romance Languages he used to attend? He was quite sought-after at one time, an associate of the great Salzer and, people said, an old buddy of Robbe-Grillet. He was one of the first to translate the work of Etienne Balibar.

Uwe was of medium height and rather slender. His walk was rather noticeable, though. He would stride with his body at an oblique angle, the left shoulder lifted and leading, and the right arm swinging in military fashion. He was always stunningly dressed, his clothes having that sheen of expensive newness. He was well-dressed at a time when profs were generally following student trends and going blue-jeaned and sweat-shirted. Often Uwe would carry his Burberry or London Fog simply over his shoulders in the Italian way, and he wore his felt hats at a slightly crooked angle, not what one would call jaunty; no, rather mildly humorous. And his eyes stressed the tinge of aristocratic humour he projected. They were so brown one could not distinguish the pupil from the rest. The whites were flawlessly white. To me his eyes seemed to be forever sparkling in the enjoyment of some secret inner expressivity.

His face was small but finely moulded, his nose straight, and his skin poreless and even: I never once saw him with the hint of a five o'clock shadow. Monica told me that the skin of his whole body was remarkably smooth and unblemished for a man, and was fully tanned — no bathing-suit whiteness. She was right. I remember how in the beginning she described his shoulders as boyishly muscular, his calves hard, as were his buttocks, but that he had something of an emerging pot-belly, undetectable when he was dressed. Yes, he had all that too.

I first saw Uwe Wenzel in performance when I sat in on a panel dealing with the ongoing influence of the *commedia dell'arte* on contemporary Italian drama, and I was impressed by the florid yet witty way he spoke of choreographic subtleties. Monica and I were together at that conference, sharing a room in a small smelly hotel four underground stops from the conference hotel — a Sheraton or Hyatt or Hilton, I've forgotten which. No, I have not forgotten. How could I forget? It was a Hilton and it was too expensive for us.

There Monica and I were, two young assistant profs from Sebastian's Point, keen to find topics for our own original articles, anxious to be accepted by and to get on first name terms with established people, and still green enough to believe we had to fill all available conference time sitting in on panels. At night we would be loud, giggly and unfocused-eyed with exhaustion as we drank our cheap wine, sprawled over the old tobacco-infused spreads on our narrow beds, insisting that it *was* Carl Sandburg who had once lived in this hotel, and dreaming out loud with hiccups about how famous we would become when we had tugged out of our theoretic consciousness the fantastic insights we knew were lurking there stubbornly.

But this is not a story about the conference circuit. It's about the effect of Uwe Wenzel on Monica and me.

I remember our meeting clearly because I was envious of the attention Uwe paid to Monica while ignoring me. I mean, I was the one who had gone to hear him deliver his paper and had asked him the only question he got from the floor.

Monica and I had crashed the Washington party on the last night, and we were beaming with I-don't-give-a-fuckism at each other as we sipped their expensive champagne and admired each other's good little black dresses. Monica did look nice, I had to admit. Her face was plump and her head rather large for the size of her body, but her lips were full and her smile wide and challenging. When she put on eye make-up, her eyes looked mysterious but not dauntingly so. And she had thick, naturally curly black hair that dandelioned around her face. I, however, have fair hair, hair so limp and straight that it sits around my face like two sheets of damp paper. I have never liked my looks much, my narrow compact body. But I do recall in ballet class when I was a high school freshman, a large fattish unco-ordinated girl saying to me, 'You tidy little blondes are so goddamn lucky. I hate you all.'

We had just downed our first glass of champagne when Uwe approached us. He looked at our name tags and then into Monica's eyes. '*Where* is Sebastian's Point?' he asked.

'You don't really want to know, do you?' she replied, her eyes on him like friendly Russian Ikons.

'Ah, but perhaps I do, my dear. I am Uwe Wenzel. It is my pleasure.' He bowed slightly, holding out his hand to her, and his eyes gleamed like polished garnets or ripe dates. I imagined touching them with the tip of my tongue (though perhaps it was later that I had that fantasy. I had many fantasies about Uwe Wenzel over the next year or so).

He held onto Monica's hand, complimenting her in Italian on her dress. She replied in an accent as perfect as his. He pursed his lips with pleasure, in a kind of inverted smile, and touched her upper arm briefly with a smooth, muscled hand. Monica cleverly then, without gushing, let him know she knew his work on Balibar. I saw I was not wanted. 'I'm going to get more champagne,' I said quickly, and left before Uwe decided gallantly to fetch the champagne for me.

I was standing alone at the cash-bar when Monica came up to me hurriedly. 'Tania,' she said, looking ashamed and yet excited, 'do you mind if I go with Uwe Wenzel for dinner? I know we planned ... but this is our last night, and he is so interesting. Actually ... would you like to join us?' This last sentence was mouthed with such high-pitched falsity that I thought, Monica, go jump in the goddamn lake. 'No thanks, Mon,' I said. 'Quite candidly, I do not want to join the two of you at dinner. You run along and enjoy yourself. I'll see you back later at the hotel. Don't forget our plane leaves at eleven and we'll have to check out at nine.'

'I won't, honestly. See you later. And sorry to desert you like this.' Her face dropped with remorse. 'It's a rotten thing to do. Look, I'll tell him I can't ...'

'Go and have dinner,' I said, pushing her away, my jaw tight.

Monica did not come back to the hotel at all that night. She phoned me there at around 11:30 to let me know that she'd meet me at the airport next morning, and would I bring her things with me. 'Tania, I'm having such a wonderful time,' she said so softly I had to assume he was close by. 'He's terrific, and he knows everything and everybody.'

Alone in the gloomy green-painted room, with its rattling radiators, gurgling plumbing, and a window that looked onto an eroded brick wall, I read myself into tiredness, unable to remove or dissolve a sense of betrayal, a feeling like something I had swallowed and that had settled low in my throat.

I need to remind you for my own and Monica's sake that this all started in the winter of 1974 when jobs were hard to get and when a practical feminism, sometimes unsure of its own dicta, was fighting for existence. Though, on a campus like Sebastian's Point, at the back of the beyond in Vermont, feminism was only a kind of underground conversation not strong enough to deconstruct the students' or the faculty's thinking. Or mine and Monica's for that matter. We both expected men to want to come on to us, to want to take us to bed. We both expected to live lives with men to some extent conventionally. So I was not at all surprised when Monica told me the things she did, in a low voice, as we sat together in the plane going home, in a placid mood of intimacy and projection.

'We had the most wonderful time in this Greek restaurant. It was so ornate, you wouldn't believe it. Carved vines climbing over pedestals, and blue baby angels and philosophers' laurel-wreathed heads everywhere. And it was so empty that Uwe and I had three waiters all to ourselves. They stood to one side, though, and didn't stare at us, which I hate. I hate it when waiters watch every mouthful one takes. But they would sweep the plates away as we finished, and they kept the wine glasses filled, and it was so royal you know, and so glamorous. Then he said we should drive a little out of the city to a hillock he knew near some old cloisters from which there was a view. I just remember how easily he pulled me to him, how smoothly. Then, almost snakily, his hand moved up my dress and down into my pants. You know, it was as if he knew my ... my topography.' Monica laughed breathily. 'My geography. He was so expert. He is ... he is a sort of all-round genius,' she added. I wanted to say, Come on Monica, gimme a break. 'Well then, we decided I should telephone you and spend the night with him at the Hilton. Tania, I do really appreciate your handling all the baggage ...'

She sat back in her seat, sated, happy and relaxed in the droning of the plane. I looked at the cotton-ball clouds beyond the window and hated my own resentment.

Over the next year Monica persistently showed me, even as I turned my head aside, the letters Uwe wrote her, and told me about the late-night calls. After her first visit to his house in the spring break, she became almost solemn in her search for the right words to describe the slippery pleasure of satin sheets, or his piquant breaking-off of love-making just when she was truly roused so that he could bring them chilled wine from the fridge, and the *Arabian* selection of perfumes and powders he provided her with in the vast bathroom with its sunken double bath. Breakfast might consist of many little courses: strawberries in Kirsch, for instance; Russian eggs in aspic, tiny squares of toast with caviar and shallots, hot moist paniottas, soft orange gellato, chestnuts surrounded by lean bacon, and lots and lots of little cups of Swedish coffee.

I found myself split between a voyeuristic desire to see her experiences with my mind's eye, and a dread of the longing and jealousy these same experiences would rouse in me. The jealousy made me want to cut her down, insult her, call her the Whore of Academe, the Toady of Italian Studies. Such insults could always have been turned into jokes if Monica's anger had been hard to confront. I could have played on words while hating her. But finally I did not dare.

Shortly before the next summer vacation, Monica and I had a celebratory dinner together. We had both learnt that we would be kept on for another year at Sebastian's Point; I had a grant to work on my Montale book; and Monica was to spend time with Uwe, first in Seattle and then on vacation on the island of Sylt in the North Sea.

'Everyone on Sylt sunbathes in the nude,' she informed me, spooning rock lobster carefully into her mouth, her eyes gleaming with what I was sure was a pretended naughtiness. 'And all the European film stars go there.'

'So what?'

'Well, don't you think that's exciting?'

'No.'

'I mean, when last did any lovely sleazy glamour come our way at this campus, hey? Besides, the thought of lying on warm seasand naked, with Uwe naked, excites me.'

'Oh shut up!'

'Tania! What's up with you?'

'It annoys me to see you so ... so taken with that Uwe that you have forgotten who you are ... a serious woman ... a scholar ...'

'Tania, I am serious.' She looked serious. She put down her fork and put her hand on mine.

'You are so in love, frankly, it's sickening,' I said, but returned the pressure of her hand. 'The guy's twenty years older than you and most of the year he lives about two thousand miles away, and ...'

'Age doesn't matter, Tania,' Monica said in an aunt-like fashion. 'Neither age, nor time, nor space.'

I had to laugh, then so did she. We got caught in the laughing and only stopped when we noticed other diners looking at us. 'Let's get on with the meal,' I said.

When Monica returned from Sylt at the end of the summer, she was thinner, tanned, and her thick hair had been cut very short, giving her the look of a Mediterranean androgyne. Her face showed a spirited sort of excitement over more than simply having had a vacation that was an onslaught of sensuality (her term). She had a new project. Uwe had got her interested in attempting a biography of Elisabetta Pierroti. Pierroti had been a popular novelist in the forties but was now living in seclusion in Lecce. She was old and ailing, but Uwe had heard that her novels were about to be republished in English translation by a newly established feminist press. He urged Monica to interview Pierroti and her family, dig up any available secondary material, and *get writing*. If she could complete her book so that its appearance coincided with the appearance of the novels, it might get a lot of critical attention. So Uwe said.

'What about your work on Pavese?'

'Uwe doesn't think it's moving along fast enough. He doesn't think it's original, really.'

'I don't agree! But in any case you know nothing about the writing of biography, Monica. Or will Uwe write it for you too?'

'Tania, don't be such a bitch. I could learn enough about biographic writing between now and next spring to make a start ... when I get back from Italy.'

'Italy? You're going to Italy? With what money?'

'With Uwe's.' Her eyes lowered and her mouth thinned. When she looked up, her eyes were steady. 'I *must* do this, Tania. It could be the break I need. Uwe says ...'

'Okay, okay, do it. Do it. Just don't quote Uwe to me once more today.'

We walk naked on Sylt, hand in hand, he talking of Moravia's stupidities and laughing at Pasolini's supernatural natural comedies. He lets us become two minds and mouths, talking, joined, lip on lip, my hip to his thigh. He has no separation, no division of body, mind and soul. He gulps at the goblet of bubbles as he does my body in its panting of breath and salt water, and he recites Dante's cadenced lines. Wake up, Tania, you are eavesdropping in your sleep.

Our second snowfall had settled in and the winds from Canada we dreaded were blowing, when Monica took off for Italy. She was well-prepared for her task, having read Pierroti's novels in the original, and carrying letters of introduction to writers and literati who might be of help — provided by Uwe.

She was in a state of unusual restless tension as I drove her to the airport, shifting in her seat, doing and undoing the seatbelt, telling me to drive faster and then to watch where I was going. Tania, careful for that truck! Is that a cop-car ahead? If we miss this flight ... I should have stuck to my work on Pavese. I'm sure the plane won't be able to take off with this snow on the ground. Italy in April will be awful, remember *The Wings of a Dove* ...'

Uwe Wenzel knew everyone in Romance Language Studies who counted for anything. And, as I have shown, he had become a reference point for both of us (for me to my shame). Our professional lives were regularly punctuated with the question, What would Uwe think? He might have been our god, but he could not know everything. He could not know that Elisabetta Pierroti, as old and infirm as she was, would decide to write her autobiography when interest in republishing her books in English was shown. She bought a dictaphone and employed one of her nieces as typist. She began dictating a full half-year before Monica approached her for an interview, but said nothing to anyone about it: perhaps she feared that this, her last book, might not get finished.

So it was not surprising that Monica returned rather discouraged and nonplussed from her pilgrimage to Lecce.

'What a strange old woman,' Monica complained. 'It's hard to believe she's a writer, she's so reticent, so *wordless*. She lives in this old stone farmhouse with a couple of nieces who look like spinsters out of an old Antonioni movie. *They* wouldn't speak, except to say hello and goodbye. Pierroti herself seemed to be wearing the very dresses she bought in her heyday, and she obviously did not want to discuss her life or her writing with me at all. I mean, geez, I travel all the way to the mob-city of Lecce to get to speak to her, but she won't speak!'

'Didn't she speak at all?'

'Oh, she answered some questions but very briefly. She gave me a tour of her house and then handed this to me.' Monica showed me a typed sheet consisting of a list of dates with a dry sentence or two attached to each. A terse and therefore tantalizing chronology.

Two days later, however, Monica was in a state of annoying creative euphoria. She was going to use the chronology to start writing her book, but was now going to structure it as a novel. We were in my office when she started telling me her plans, and I had to get up and move, I became so agitated. I went to stand at the window, looking out at the mediocre architecture, blurred but not improved by snow flurries.

'Everyone writes novelistic biographies these days,' she said defensively.

'What will Uwe say?'

'As long as the job's well done, he won't mind.'

'Did Pierroti give you any sort of authorization?'

'No. But she did not say I *couldn't* write about her.'

'But you don't have much to go on.'

'That's why I have to write a novel. And I'll do the best I can. And don't forget a large part of the book will be a discussion, coming from the thoughts of the writer, of the novels themselves, and I'll show how what she was writing linked up with what she was experiencing at the time.'

'Well, your mind is obviously made up, but I think you're biting off more than you can chew.'

'You are *so* discouraging.'

'Well, I'm sorry.'

'Tania, I have to get writing.'

I knew that Monica and Uwe had spoken of marriage, but it was then that I wondered whether the marriage depended on Monica's producing a publishable book. Appalled and yet sourly fascinated, I looked into her appealing dark eyes.

When the second of Pierroti's novels appeared in English, Monica decided to place a biographic article in a literary journal. It was a lovely essay, shaded with tender vignettes, mood pieces, and poetic descriptions. For instance, the opening lines read: Under the mauve skies of a gardenia-scented Italian dusk, two women walk hand in hand, talking in low voices, the younger supporting the older one as they linger among ancient knotted olive trees.

Later in the piece, Monica mentioned the psychiatrist who had treated Pierroti at her family's insistence when she had wanted to retreat to the farmhouse outside Lecce. Monica described the golden glow in the booklined study and the rich red of the drapes tinting the noble forehead of Dr Sandro Sdoya. As I read, I wondered why Monica had trusted the diagnosis of not only a male but an old Freudian. Sdoya spoke with a gruff voice but one resonant with compassion (she wrote) for what he called Pierroti's 'Presenile psychosis', her agoraphobia, and his inability to get her to let him help her. Monica evoked movingly, too, Elisabetta's desertion by her husband and her sorrow at never having had a child of her own. Monica suggested that Elisabetta had implied that she, Monica, was like the daughter she had never had.

The journal that published Monica's essay sent a copy to Elisabetta Pierroti.

The summer vacation lay two weeks ahead. I was sitting on a bench under a red beech, grading papers, and enjoying the sunny, not-too-warm, pre-mosquito season, when I saw Monica loping across the grass toward me. She had a heavy run, each foot clinging to the earth as if unwilling to leave it. As she got closer, I saw that her eyes were wide with a brilliant happiness.

'Uwe's arriving tonight,' she called. 'He phoned. He's getting a flight this afternoon, well, this morning his time, and he'll be here at six. He says he needs to talk to me urgently. Face-to-face.' She sank down on the bench next to me and hugged my arm to her cheek. 'Oh, I look so forward to seeing him ...' I wanted to ask her how long he would stay, and I wondered whether there would be a lunch or dinner I might be invited to as well. But I shut my mouth and felt her warmth through my sleeve.

I never did discover where they went or what they did that night. The next day I caught a glimpse of them walking along the tree-lined road in front of our apartment building. They were not arm in arm. I studied the back of Uwe's head, the Soviet swing of his arm, and the breadth of shoulder in a tweed jacket. I waited for them to turn so that I could see his face, but they went on. What was Uwe thinking of Monica's essay? What was he saying? What about … could he be discussing my articles on Montale? You are a snake, I told myself. Or a jinx. Could you have willed it all, I was later to ask myself.

The next afternoon my doorbell rang with the continuousness of someone leaning on it. I let Monica up. Her face was so mottled, she looked drunk.

'Monica?'

'I can't believe it! I can't honestly believe it!' she gasped, the hollows of her throat tightening and swelling, and tightening again. She handed me a book with a stiff glossy dust jacket. The title read: Elisabetta Pierroti: *Una Nuova Vita Vecchia*.

'What's this?' I asked.

'Can't you see?'

'What? Oh … my … God. Monica, come in. Sit down.'

She threw herself onto my couch as if she had been shot in the back. She beat her head against a cushion as I paged through the book, Pierroti's autobiography in Italian.

On page xiv of the introduction, Pierroti referred to Monica's essay, accusing her of unprofessional behaviour. She stated that for the past five years she had suffered from a bone disease that made it impossible for her to walk, whether supported by a younger woman or not. In a long paragraph she detailed the damage that Dr Sandro Sdoya had done her in his patriarchal form of snake-medicine. She castigated her family for wanting her to conform to the norm of the Italian housewife or overworked spinster. She pointed out that she had left her husband after three months' marriage because of his violence, and stated with passion that she had been born in 1912 (I am not quoting her exactly), had lived through the worst of Italian fascism, had survived the war, and had decided the world was no place for children. She ended her reference to Monica's essay by insisting that any further discussion of herself or her work by Professor Monica Styles was to be regarded as inexact. 'Everything Professor Styles has to say about me is either a gross distortion or an invention.' So ended the paragraph.

'Oh … my … God,' I repeated.

'I am finished,' moaned Monica into the pillow. 'My life is finished …'

'Where did you get this book?' I asked, growing tense with bitter joy and yet as sad as a mother whose child has been hurt by outsiders.

'Uwe brought it.' Monica sort of coughed and then broke down.

He wanted no further relationship with her. He had even brought a document prepared by a lawyer which he asked Monica to sign. It declared that any contract between them to marry was thereby cancelled.

I went to sit on the floor at the couch. Monica cried like a child, her fists clutching the cushion. I dared not touch her, nor, I knew, was I called upon to speak. In any case, I could not make much sense of my own cluster of feelings, predominant of which was a sense of peace, of something having been consummated and therefore concluded. Yet I had the impulse to cry too, in part for Monica but mostly because of the huge all-encompassing ectoplasm-like dome that seemed to be the situation of our professional lives. We could push against it and it might give, but the fabric would never tear. We were caught.

After a while Monica's rawly exhaled sobs made me want to laugh. 'Come on, Mon,' I said firmly while swallowing

103

hard, 'come let's go and get a drink.' She sat up and rubbed her mottled face with her hands. I closed the book I still held, placing the document inside the front cover. 'Let's go across to Brubaker's,' I suggested.

'Yeah, let's go …' She stood, swayed a little, then went to the bathroom to wash her face.

We ordered double shots of Absolut on ice. Monica's face had regained its normal creamy colour, except for the eyes which were red and thick-lidded, her gaze resigned, aged. 'What are your plans for the summer?' she asked me.

'Monica, let's not talk shop.'

'You're going to finish your Montale book, aren't you?'

'Whatever,' I said, concentrating on the bright hard cleansing effect of the liquor, but Monica was staring at me intently so I played along. 'So, you're going to continue work on that biographic novel?'

'I don't know …' Then more loudly she declared, 'Yes, I am going to finish it, come hell or high water. But order me another drink.' Smiling, but a little exasperated, I motioned to the waitress.

'You still want to write a novel?'

'Yes, a novel, a *lurid* novel. Now that her autobiography is out I'll have more to go on and more to distort. But I'm also going to resign my job.'

'What?'

'Yes, I'm pulling out.'

'After all those years of study and, what, five years at Sebastian's Point? Don't do it!'

'I've decided.' She took the glass almost from the waitress's hand. 'And here's to … to unprofessional conduct and freedom!'

The following year my own book on Montale did come out and to decent reviews. Monica had meanwhile gone back to her old home town in northern Illinois where she joined her sister in running a realtor's office. But she found time to finish a novel based on Pierroti's life. I thought it rather good, and it's since come out in paperback. For two weeks it even stood on supermarket shelves.

The next winter I was at a meeting on *The Image of the Italian in American Literature*. I was sitting in one of those fat armchairs large hotels have in their foyers when I saw the elevator doors open and Uwe Wenzel step out. He saw me. He wore a black overcoat casually over a smooth grey suit, a red carnation in his buttonhole, and he was holding one of those small leather handbags so useful to men but which only Europeans feel they can carry without their masculinity being doubted.

He headed toward me, his eyes bright as marbles and humorously questioning. I knew his first words would be a compliment on my book and his second a comment on the Claiborne suit I was wearing. More ready than he realized, I stood up and waited as, swinging his right arm, he descended upon me.

RUNNING NAKED

One evening in the spring of 1952, in a dusk of fresh wind and even grey-blue light, a worker stepped out of the Bailey Welding Company, a shop built on the banks of the Monongahela River, in among the Pittsburgh steelmills. He wanted a cigarette away from the noise and stench of the floor and to enjoy the last light of the first day of good weather.

At first it seemed noiseless out-of-doors after the incessant clanging indoors. Then he became aware of the calls of free-wheeling birds playful over the treetops, and the drone of home-going traffic on the bridge to his left. Relaxed, standing with legs straddled, he smoked slowly but deeply.

There was a grinding rumble overhead. He looked at his watch. It was after six, a busy time for planes landing and taking off at the local airport. Though, he couldn't recall ever hearing one this loud before. It must be flying lower than usual. Suddenly the plane was there directly over him, suspended just above the roof of the workshop, rocking like a shark confused by a too-tight line. He had never in his life, even in Europe in the war, seen a plane so low or felt that he could reach up and touch the sectioned underbelly. Then the plane's engines shut off and his ears blocked with the sudden silence. Unnerved, the man let his cigarette slip from his fingers as he watched the machine dive and come to a shocking slapping landing on the surface of the Monongahela River.

For a moment the plane floated pendulously, and he was sure he could make out startled faces at the windows. He wanted to call out but his throat had closed. He did not notice that some of his buddies had come outside to stare. Nose downward, the plane slowly submerged, the brown water of the river parting for its long body and drawing it in with a monstrous sucking sound.

The plane was gone. The river water, lurching and pitching against its banks, settled over it. None of the workers moved.

That night the man, Jeff Hughes, told his wife Merrilyn what he had seen. He spoke so matter-of-factly that he suspected she thought he was making up the story. But because he felt over-excited, even jittery, he had kept his voice even. He half-smiled as he spoke, and smoked with a new wrist-flicking sophistication, waiting for Merrilyn's face to open with horror and astonishment. Only when the story was broadcast on the radio at nine did she fully believe him. All she could say was, Poor people. Poor, poor people. And he felt that his role as witness had not been important in her eyes.

But that was just like her, he reminded himself. She had never showed much interest in listening to stories, not even the unimaginable ones about the war he had tried telling her more than once.

The plane was never found. For days hundreds of people came to the river banks and obstructed traffic on the bridge as divers tried to locate the craft. For nearly two weeks its disappearance was front-page news in Pennsylvania papers and fourth-page news elsewhere. Editorials speculated that when the pilot realized he was in trouble, he had tried to land on the river, hoping the plane would float long enough for some to be rescued. That was a plausible explanation. Where the plane was brought down was the only unobstructed stretch of river, several bridges spanning the water beyond that. And, certainly, there was no flat land in the area where he could have attempted a crash-landing without destroying the lives of those who, like Jeff, lived on the plateaus rising up from the river.

The plane was gone. It had disappeared entirely, drawn down into the mud of the river, pulled into another dimension. No passengers, no pilot, no crew; no body was ever recovered. The only aftermath, apart from speculation, was an award for bravery given to the pilot's wife on his behalf almost concurrently with his first pension check.

Coming and going across the bridge daily, Jeff would stop and gaze at the river's seemingly slow-moving surface and wonder exactly how the people in the cabin had died. Did water seep in and drown them as they tried to claw their way to the ceiling? Did they die of suffocation, slowly slumping tear-stained to the floor? Or, as the plane felt the weight of the mud, did it groaningly squeeze apart at the seams, drawing in huge folds of icy sludge to engulf the bodies?

Jeff started having dreams. He was in a darkening plane, cries in his ears and hot, bitter smells in his nostrils. He was losing his breath to encroaching heat and airlessness. He opened his mouth to call but his tongue cleaved to his palate. Crouching in his seat, hugging his knees, the seat-belt biting into his waist, his body would begin to go into spasms, and then his shuddering would wake him. He would have to sit up in bed and breathe deeply to calm himself. Then he would reach for his cigarettes on the night-table.

If his dreaming had not woken Merrilyn, the scratch of the match would. She would try speaking soothingly to him but her voice only increased his terrible sense of unease. Once she laid a soft warm palm on his forehead, but he brushed her hand away. Her feelings were wounded. Their six-year marriage had always been peaceful and she had no skills to help her handle this intangible crisis. The next day she moved some things to the spare bedroom and thereafter frequently slept there. On those nights Jeff would want to ask her to return to their bed, but even as he framed the words he forgot why it mattered that they should sleep together.

Before the plane crash, Merrilyn's predictability and unchangeableness had been a kind of refuge to Jeff against a skittish world that did not meet reasonable expectations or repay hard lessons learnt. People were fickle: they liked him and then they did not. His bosses rewarded and castigated him randomly. Machinery gave in unexpectedly. His own body could not be relied on. Yet Merrilyn stayed the same. She had been a nurse before their marriage and managed to retain as a housewife the calm, clean-smelling, orderliness of her profession. She economized sensibly and yet did not allow the house or herself to become dowdy. She made her own clothes, favouring crisp, bright cottons for dresses and cable-stitch patterns for sweaters. She had not changed the patterns over the years though she had altered the prints, and she did not change the style of her short, tidily curled dark hair. She prepared their meals efficiently, and Jeff liked to know that on a Monday they ate beef stew, on a Tuesday pork chops, on a Wednesday hamburgers, and so on. Up until the plane crash, he had been comforted by her undeviating thrifty sameness, her unruffled demeanour, and her commonsensical conversations.

After the plane crash he found himself daunted at times by her assumption of timelessness, within and without herself. Her impassivity seemed no longer a protection for him but a facade which, in its very mildness and cheerfulness, could attract disaster to his own home. Once, surprising himself, he looked across their living-room at her as she sat tranquilly knitting, and grew sullen. He wanted to say something harsh, deliver a warning perhaps, that would shock her out of her composure. Instead, he got up abruptly and went to stand in the dark at the garden gate. By the movement of light behind him he knew that she had risen and was staring at him through the window.

On another evening as they sat quietly sharing sections of the newspaper after dinner, she asked in the flat voice she used when she wanted to disguise anxiety:

'Jeff, why didn't you finish your food? You usually enjoy my fried chicken. And you didn't touch your pie ...'

'I wasn't very hungry.'

'You must be getting tired of my cooking.'

'I like your cooking.'

'You haven't been sleeping well lately. And you're withdrawn. What's the matter?'

'Nothing. I've got stuff on my mind.'

'I think maybe we've got into a rut.'

'No, we haven't.'

'We should go out more. We should go back to bowling on Tuesdays. Remember how much you used to like bowling?'

'Yeah, maybe we could go back to bowling.'

'We should get some brochures from the travel agent and think about a vacation, and I should try some new recipes ...'

'No, no, don't ...' Jeff, feeling annoyance at having to talk when he would rather have remained silent and thoughtful, got up, folded his piece of newspaper and handed it to Merrilyn. His mind, changing immediately from irritated to preoccupied, he went down to the basement where his workbench and old desk stood.

Jeff was not an educated man, but he was a good welder and, at thirty, had retained from his schooldays a talented and exact knowledge of mathematics. Some days after the crash, he had made sketches of planes seen from different angles on large sheets of butcher's paper. Now, standing at his desk, he stared down at the sketches. He asked himself how the plane would have needed to be modified so that the pilot could have floated it on the water long enough for rescuers to have got to work. That evening and the two following ones, when again he had not finished his dinner, he set himself the task of redesigning an airplane's underbelly.

On the fourth evening, he returned from Bailey's Welding in a pink twilight that sweetened faces and dispositions, and lent grace to the outlines of wire fences, walls, gutters, and the dandelions dotting his now unkempt front lawn. The quality of the light softened him and something of his previous contentment returned. But when unusual cooking smells came from the kitchen as he entered his house, he felt vaguely alarmed. He went through to the kitchen to greet Merrilyn but, instead, stared uncertainly at her as she stood at the stove stirring and stirring something in a saucepan. She looked different, in which way he was not immediately sure. Not as well-groomed, perhaps. A little flushed. Her apron hung limp and streaked as if desperate sticky hands had rubbed themselves constantly down it.

'What are you doing?' he asked.

'I'm reducing.'

'What d'you mean?'

'I'm thickening this sauce.'

'What are you making?'

'Some new recipes.'

'But you know I don't like new things. Not all of a sudden.'

'For once we should try something a bit exotic, don't you think?'

'Exotic? I dunno …'

At table Jeff forked some pinkish yellow rice. 'What did you put in the rice?' he asked. Fragments of green leaf patterned it.

'It's called saffron risotto,' said Merrilyn. 'It's got saffron and dry wine and basil in it. Do you like it?'

'What's saffron?'

'It's a … a spice, I think. Do you like the veal?'

'Is that what this is? It's kinda pale.'

'Yes, well, it should be. But the sauce has butter, cream, sherry, cumin and black pepper in it, and …'

He tasted it. 'It must've taken you a long time to cook,' he said, sounding begrudging. He cut and bit a piece of veal. It had a pleasant, tender resilience against his teeth, and the sauce was at the same time tart and sweet. He looked up, uncertain how to respond. Again he was distracted by Merrilyn's appearance. Her hair had escaped from the usual orderly rows of curls and frizzed in corkscrew filaments around her face. Strands clung to her neck and a whorl had sprung up at the top of her head.

'What's wrong with your hair?' he asked.

'Oh,' she said, tucking wisps behind her ears. 'I didn't have time to set it in rollers. I haven't had time to curl it.'

'But it is curly. *Very* curly.'

'Yes, but not *set* curls. This is its natural curliness. Which I hate.'

She looked down, frowning, and continued eating as Jeff studied her. She was unlike herself. She looked wild. She did not seem aware that a button had come undone at the back of her blouse and that the neckline had shifted, showing a bra-strap over one pale shoulder. And, although her hand held her fork with delicate curled fingers, she was eating rather fast and greedily. Jeff ate more of his veal, trying to duplicate in himself Merrilyn's preoccupation with the food, her hungry intensity.

Then dessert came, a custardy mixture he did not care for and which she called a *Sauterne sabayon*, and spooned smoothly into her mouth, her gaze turned inward and not, as it always was at table, focused on him. Jeff was nonplussed.

Wanting to punish her for springing the unforeseen on him, for apparently reading his mind but exaggerating his annoyance at her predictability, he refused to sit reading the newspaper with her over coffee, but went down to the basement to stare at his designs with unseeing eyes. How disconcerting, he thought, to discover after several years of marriage that your wife had naturally tightly curly hair. But how could he have known this when every morning she wound her hair into rollers and covered it with a scarf, and when once a week she went to the beauty shop? Why had she never mentioned hating her hair, and why had he been so unobservant? Why had she never revealed her interest in strange-tasting foods? What else about herself was she hiding from him? He shuddered. He was being childish. Hair, foods — these were harmless things. Not like the random catastrophes that could maim or kill human beings.

He concentrated on his design. A growing excitement made him forget his wife's surprises and even his need to smoke after a meal. He took up a pencil and continued working on an airliner's undercarriage that would have an ejectable segment. When the pilot ejected this portion (at this stage Jeff was not sure how), the plane's belly became concave. Jeff visualized that at the same time a small propeller under each wing would become activated, providing an air-cushion as the plane came to rest on water. In this way any plane in trouble could stay afloat indefinitely. Or so he theorized. He wished he knew more about aerodynamics and engineering. He wished his math skills were greater than they were. He wanted to go down in history as the man who invented means to prevent planes ever again sinking down into mud or breaking apart on the rocks and reefs under the sea.

Hours later, feeling tired but also calmly happy from the conviction that he was onto an important discovery, Jeff came up from the basement. The lights were off except for the living-room lamp and the outside light. Merrilyn had gone to bed, again in the spare room. Not wanting to sleep yet himself, he walked softly through the house and out to the front garden. There he stood and looked up at the sky. The night was clear and warm and still, and in spite of the haze from the mills he could see the stars and the regular pulsing lights of a plane way overhead. There was not much traffic about so he decided to walk down to the river.

At the railing on the bridge he stopped to rest and light a cigarette. There was no breeze and the only sound he registered was the purling of the water moving blackly under the bridge. In his mind's eye he could see the plane deep below, submerged in mud, its shiny metal rusted and tarnished, the windows fogged over from inside and out. His mood of satisfaction shifted and so he paced a bit, trying to remind himself that he had a huge task ahead and should not become discouraged. He must rework his drawings as clearly as he could and then take the sheets to either the Patents Pending Office in the city or at least to show them to a mechanical engineer at the university and ask for advice. But could he trust such a person not to steal his ideas? No. Well, the Patents Pending Office would be better.

Jeff flicked the red-tipped stub into the water and drew another cigarette out of the pack. Then he replaced it in his upper shirt pocket and headed back toward home.

Along a steep narrow street close to his house, he suddenly became aware of running feet. He hesitated and then edged against a tree trunk, afraid of thugs and hoping that he was hidden by the dense shadowy overhang. He heard high-pitched calls and then saw a woman sprinting down the opposite sidewalk. Had the sound of her feet on the concrete paving not been so clear, he might have thought he was seeing things. The woman was, apart from her shoes, stark naked. Her breasts bobbed as she passed under a street light, and her hair waved behind her. Jeff was about to step out from under the tree and offer her assistance, when a naked man came jogging after her. His genitals swung slightly, and as they both went by, their buttocks flickered in the lamplight. Their voices, high and delighted in banter and laughter, made it clear no one was menacing or trying to escape the other. Yet Jeff's heart was thumping heavily and he had to put his fingers up to his mouth to hold the trembling of his lips.

When the runners were out of sight, he came away from the tree and sat on the sidewalk, his body shaking and his mind peculiarly shocked. He felt the impulse to laugh and a tightening of his stomach muscles, but then had to lift his head up and back so that the tears that came to his eyes could not drip down. Sonnovabitch, he murmured. Sonnovabitch.

When the plane had landed on the Monongahela River, the sight had been so enormous, so unbelievable, that he had not had time for the shaking fear he had felt a few moments ago. That the plane would sink so soon had been a shock that had at first enthralled rather than frightened him. But those runners were different. Their nakedness had seemed very vulnerable to attack and yet at the same time, he now realized, threatening. And in their flagrant disregard for law, convention, modesty, they constituted elements in an extensive and finely woven mesh of random occurrences that menaced his life.

What had he left to rely on? Jeff asked himself. He had once thought himself a lucky man for hadn't he got through the last days of a world war unscathed? But these days and in his own home town, he was forced to witness immense disasters, inexplicable human idiosyncrasies, and a wife who had grown unfamiliar.

He sat staring up at a street lamp until his eyes projected red and green flashes in its shape. He smoothed back his hair and got to his feet. It was time he got home to bed.

By the time he got to his house, Jeff was laughing a little, cursing the runners roundly. Really, some people! One had no idea what nonsense one's neighbours would get up to. He wished Merrilyn were still awake so that he could tell her what he had seen and have them both laugh about it. He even decided that he would like to tell her how the plane crash had been absorbing his waking and sleeping thoughts. He would like to discuss his hopes of inventing a revolutionary kind of underbelly for future planes. She must have seen his drawings in the basement and wondered what they were.

At home he went to pour himself some milk. In the fridge's yellow light he saw medallions of some sort of meat marinating in a herbal-smelling liquid. Another new recipe. He would have to eat more heartily and suggest with more interest that Merrilyn again serve him on occasion grilled steak and hamburger. Praise the new stuff but beg for the old. Suddenly a new question caused Jeff to stand at the open fridge, milk in hand, unaware of the motor kicking in as the refrigerator worked to cope with the warm air filling its interior. *Why* hadn't some brilliant aero-engineer already come up with a device to allow ordinary planes, not seaplanes, to land on water? Would such a device not be economically viable? How many planes had crashed on water?

Placing his milk on top of the fridge and closing the door, he went through to the living-room where his encyclopedias stood tightly packed in the bookcase that had come with them. He very seldom used them and the almost moist leather bindings were adhering the books the one to the other. He tugged out the Aalto/Arithmetic volume and turned to *Airline Disasters*. He carried the open book to the dining-room table and sat down to read the entry carefully.

He read down one column, then went up to the next. Airfreighters, airscouts and biplanes; cropdusters, mailplanes and turbo-props. He felt as if he were seated on top a control-tower and the heavens churned with Kitty Hawks, Fokkers, De Havilands and STOLS, here and there randomly falling, exploding in reds and oranges; some colliding into the Himalayas, the Pyrennees, and the Rockies — all on the horizon of his vision. He read about inexplicable crashes where all on board were killed but no explanation for the disasters ever coming to light: at Tashkent and Windhoek, at

117

Darwin, Brazzaville and Brno, at Seattle and Omaha. B-52s crashed into the English Channel and a Fairchild-Hiller coming in to land at Honolulu fell into the Pacific. But the air crashes in aviation history took place predominantly on land.

That must be why no one had perfected a design to make crashing on water safe. Jeff sat back to rub his eyes and erase the swirling images of aircraft on fire.

Enough, enough. He had wasted enough of his time: on a good idea, yes, but one that was not realizable, he now understood. The weeks' long heaviness on his shoulders lifted and he felt as if he were returning to his own life, gratefully, from a strange journey. He got up, put the book away and retrieved his now tepid milk from the top of the fridge. He poured it into the sink. He went down to the basement and looked at his drawings and calculations. He smoothed them out lovingly. He cherished them. Yes, he admired them. One day he would work on them again — for the hell of it. But now he would roll them up and stack them in a safe dry spot.

Upstairs, he looked in at Merrilyn sleeping in the spare bed. She lay curled up to one side of the bed as if she were sleeping next to someone. Her hair frizzed blackly against the pillowcase, and her face was peaceful. Jeff decided that he would undress quietly and creep carefully in behind her. He settled himself next to her warmth, luxuriating in the clean smell of oatmeal and lilac that came off the skin of her back.

He slept and dreamt yet another dream of a crash, but this dream was one of stillness and weightlessness. He and Merrilyn had got out of the plane and were floating in clear bubbling blue water, their arms lightly around each other's waists. He was laughing at the way the water pulled her hair up and wide around her head, and she was laughing at his laughter. He woke up, sensing how the merriment had relaxed his chest and throat. He moved a little closer to Merrilyn's body but not too close as to disturb her. The uncontrolled hair at her neck brushed his forehead and, again, the comforting smell of her skin filled his mouth. He slept.

PERSEPHONE AND THE CAT

I wake with the song still one-two-threeing in my head, honkey-tonk waltz, and gravel-voice singing, 'You're innocent when you dream, you're innocent …' While I slept the song lightened my longing for Alex, my daughter, my gone-girl, and now I lie breathing nice and hollow and deep, and stare becalmed at the pale silk of the early morning sky stretched across the uncurtained window-pane. I feel loose-limbed, innocent; not quite ready to begin waiting.

It's Alex's tape I was listening to last night, Alex who will visit me today with her husband, a man I have never seen. In my dream of her visit, I was the child, voiceless and innocent, being embraced by my daughter-mother. Awake, I'm not quite voiceless, but my talking sounds as if I'm (like another song) bats-in-the-belfry, for the stroke that felled me punched my tongue at its roots and put my mouth in splints. So to speak. Ah, I am like a bat in more ways than one, waiting, my mind upside-down, and my flutterings pathetic. But last night I dreamed innocence.

The ginger cat appears on the window-ledge, flowing and shimmering like a small red dragon. I raise myself and try to tap a finger-nail on the glass, but my hands are like pale empty gloves and the nail slides a screech on the surface.

'Oh, that sound!' objects Matti, coming into the room.

'Titty, titty,' I say.

'Now Mrs Josephs, don't you be saying no bad words,' she laughs. She plays scales on the window with all ten fingers, but the cat turns only briefly and then looks away. It begins cleaning its left shoulder with long slow licks as if time were endless. I wonder how it got on the ledge. Perhaps from a branch of the peach tree that's begun getting small leaves, folded scraps of green cloth, and tiny fecund knoblets.

Other words Matti has taught me are Bed Food Drink Hot Cold and Bath (meaning to go to the bathroom). I say them Bey Foo Deeng Hoh Coh and Baa. Once I said Oof, meaning Food. Now that's our little joke. Matti will say, 'Mrs Josephs, it's time for oof.' Yesterday she asked me what oof we should get from the deli when Alex comes. I didn't know how to convey to her that Alex is a vegetarian. I have been practising to say Alex's name, but it still comes out Alss.

I would not wish a stroke on my worst enemy. I read a book once, years ago, when I could still read many pages at a stretch so that in time the book got read, and in that book I saw how the main character suffered a stroke. He called it being stroked by God. I never forgot that phrase. But if it was the Almighty who stroked me, then she has hands of red, molten steel and finger-nails like fire-irons. I was torched down and awoke to a body that had been hammered at the joints when I was unconscious and couldn't cry for help. My eyes still unopened, I couldn't move to rub at the places of the pain because my arms seemed trapped, pinned and wired like those of a bat mounted on wood. My belly was bloated as a bat's, and every sound rattled in my head as if my skull had become a metal box.

'That cat sure is stuck-up,' says Matti. 'I seen it at the front gate and it don't like petting.' She turns away to put the kettle on for coffee. She comes back and helps me out of bed and to my chair. She brings a soft warm cloth to wipe my face and I smell the gentle puffs of her breath: toothpaste and nicotine and cherry from her lipstick. In the movement of her arms I sense the strong angular bones encased in the warm fluid muscles, and hear the low hiss of her clothes.

From my chair at the window I can see into my neighbour's back yard, an uncared-for rectangle of uneven clumps of tough grass, yellowed in places where his dogs, Gustave and Wolfie, have pissed. How can one *not* pity dogs when one sees their eager, wordless warmth, their energetic affection? Yet these dogs make me uneasy. They are both large, deep brown animals, brothers perhaps, with short coats and that wide backleg strut some male dogs have. I'm not uneasy at the sight of the ginger cat. It'll put its head down as gracefully as a dancer's and tightrope along the gutters. Or, from the grass, it'll fling itself upward like a comic superhero at the bole of the young elm and scurry to sit, tail and ears flicking but eyes wide and innocently unfocused, as the starlings dart and swirl in cheeping objection. Or it sits, as now, on the ledge and washes itself in sweet reasonableness, for the dogs are still indoors.

Matti drapes a rug across my knees and lays a tray on top of that. 'Here's your Gerber's oatmeal and fruit puree, Mrs Josephs, and a nice cuppa coffee. While I feed you, we'll decide what to buy for Miz Alex and them's lunch.' I mumble my food as Matti spoons and wipes, and we play our game of true-or-false. Matti says, 'Tater salad?' and I nod, true. She says, 'Pasta wid black olives?' I shake my head, false. Fresh French bread, yes. And so we go on, deciding on fruit-flavoured sodas and tabouli salad and a chicken-with-walnut dish and chocolate cheese-cake, but no liver pâté, no chubs, no pastrami, but a nice limberger, and Matti, sucking in her cheeks to swallow the saliva, wipes my mouth and reaches for pen and paper. 'And wine?' she asks.

'Coh, coh,' I say.

'You want it chilled good? You got it, Mrs Josephs.' She holds my tepid coffee for me to purse lips over and asks even once again, 'Miz Alex and them coming round twelve?' I nod, yes, if the flight is on time. And I remember Alex's long thin cool knuckly hands and her laugh that moved from low to a quavering high to end in a hiccup. But how long ago was that? Will she be able to stand to kiss my crumpled-paper cheeks and have the patience to watch me mouth like an old French mime? Please, you Almighty, I say, may I not disgust her. Or him, the faceless man. I turn, fearful, to stare over Mooney's, my neighbour's, back-yard.

Whenever the dogs see the ginger cat in their territory, they bark shortly and bounce stiffly, then stand with legs straddled and necks stretched. Grinning, they watch as the cat curves, sending its fur upright, a porcupine cat baring needle teeth. They edge forward. Then, as if at a signal, they separate, one trying to edge behind while the other approaches from the side. Ginger is too quick for them. She'll drop herself onto the grass and scoot away like a snake, or leap like a frog onto the fence. 'Titty, titty, titty,' I say with my wayward tongue.

'Now you relax and snooze. I'll be back in no time,' says Matti. And I doze a bit, my eyes making black and blue cats and dogs waltzing against sunlight, so innocent, so deadly, and I jump at Mooney's screendoor slamming. I hear Gustave's yipping and whining and Wolfie's baying at their morning freedom. I sit up to watch them race around the enclosed yard and then growl and slaver as they try to bite each other in an ancient mock fight. Now Wolfie is standing panting in the shade of Mooney's garage wall, and Gustave is nipping seriously at an itch on his right fore-paw. Why doesn't the cat go away, go to its home, I wonder as it drops noiselessly from the ledge onto a grassy mound. The dogs both lift their heads and stare. Ginger stretches itself elegantly and pretends not to know that both dogs have simultaneously started moving forward. I tap the pane, Katta-katta-katta. Abruptly the cat flickers through the grass and is gone.

Who is this man Alex brings with her? She wrote that he was a tall man, and friendly, a DJ and radio ham, and I see him sitting, capturing the human voices chittering and soughing round the spinning world. My ribs tighten. I begin to suspect that this man will be a blanketing shadow between me and my child, and that what language I might have today of tongue and body and face will not reach her. Why could she not come alone? Why do I want Alex to come to me as a child and yet long for her to enfold me and comfort me, the child?

I hear Matti's footsteps on the stairs. She shoulders herself through the doorway, arms hugging parcels, her lips whistling breath, and the smell of spring grass on the cold gust that pushes indoors with her. 'We gonna have us a piggy-feast,' she pants as she places the parcels on the table whose side-leaves will be opened out for the luncheon. 'Gotta put on the dog,' she says.

Matti helps me out of my nightdress and into a velour dress in navy with a beige lace collar. It's too large for me now, but no one will notice. With a soft brush she strokes some powder on my face, and touches a tube of lipstick to my lips. She combs my hair gently, taking care not to pull it or let the comb scrape my scalp which is now, I know, as pink as a baby's and showing under the grey strands. She replaces my slippers with shoes, and dabs Cologne on my wrists and in the hollows of my elbows. Then she moves my chair so that the sun is not in my face. Now the time for waiting has begun.

When Alex first wrote that she would try to get time off from work to visit me, I day-dreamed of her sleeping in her old room and being the one who would bring me my milky coffee in bed of a morning; sitting at the foot sipping her own, her unbrushed hair a black cloud around her head, and her face plump and childish with lingering sleepiness, the smell of talcum on her skin, and her smooth thin feet crossed at the ankles, so unassuming, so delicate. I imagined she would sit on my mother's old footstool with the tapestry cover, next to my chair, one arm rested on my knees, and would read to me the way I used to read to her when she was small. But my deepest hope was that she would sit close to me, her strong slender hands holding my tremulous ones, her bright face near to mine, explaining to me that the angers of the past, the shouts on the stairs, the banging of doors, the faces hard as granite, and the despising silences had been erased from inner eyes and ears, and that only our connection, mother-daughter, daughter-mother, remained. Her presence would breathe peace into me, and then all my dreams would bring me innocence.

But they will stay at the inn on Hickory Drive, and this visit will, Alex wrote, be a good chance for her to show the husband the landscapes and lakescapes of Wisconsin, and to trace the tracks of the old fur traders and the stern-faced Jesuits. May is good weather for driving; May of slight showers and flapping wind, and the green sprinkled everywhere.

A blue-winged insect has come to bounce and tap against the window-pane, and now, immediately, the cat is here, ears stiff for a game. Coolly, with one paw, she bats at the fly but misses. In circular and triangular patterns, paw and fly dance over the pane, then Ginger, lifting herself, tries both paws, only to wobble, momentarily to regain balance, and then be forced to jump. A laugh, not quite a laugh, pulses under my ribs.

'Well, that about does it,' says Matti. 'We sure got us a fine spread, Mrs Josephs. Some real fine oof,' she laughs.

I crane and look and, yes, the table does look inviting, even festive with the wine-bottle slanting out of the ice-bucket, and the bunch of crocuses Matti has placed to one side out of the way of people serving themselves food looking stiffly fresh.

'And you're sure you want me to stay on for lunch?' asks Matti once again.

'Yeh, yeh, Maddi,' I nod. If Alex should want to feed me herself, I would be grateful, but I don't want her to *have* to do so. Besides, Matti deserves a tasty meal and a glass of wine. She is so good, so good.

I hear Gustave and Wolfie barking, a barking that takes on that rebounding repetitiveness because of something that will not go away.

'Oh, hush-up dawgs,' says Matti. But a car-door slams and then another, and Matti and I exchange glances. 'I think maybe they here,' she says, straightening her dress and heading for the door.

I wait and wait, the seconds like my heart-beats holding back my breath, and I cannot make out what the voices at the foot of the stairs are saying or why Alex doesn't come running up to me. There are too many voices, then laughter, why laughter? And only then footsteps and Matti's strong tones reaching me, 'We got enough to feed one more visitor, that's for sure ...' Matti appears first and holds the door open. Alex steps in, hesitating, to be pushed forward by two men who crowd into the room, Alex in a large trench coat, her black cut hair cut short as a boy's, her face thin, too finely molded to her cheekbones, and her tawny eyes wide on me. 'Alss, Alss ...'

'Oh, Mother, I'm so sorry about ...' She strides forward, coat flapping like the wings of a beige bird, and bends to kiss me on the right temple, her breath as I remember it, milk and mints and fruit-flavoured gum. Her hands are cool on my arms. 'Mother, how *are* you now?' I nod and nod, lifting my head back, nodding, so that the tears will not spill, and she kisses my left temple. 'Dr Heyns said it's miraculous, your recovery. I was so relieved. Mother, you must meet my husband ...' Her laugh trills and she straightens and turns. 'This is Damon, and this is David, Damon's brother who decided at the last minute he also needed a vacation.' My right hand is lifted and enfolded in the firm flesh of first one man's hand and then another, and then let fall into my lap. 'And Matti is taking good care of you?' She moves to where Matti is standing, broadly smiling, and hugs her. 'Oh, Matti!' says Alex fondly, and Matti says, 'She no trouble, no trouble at all.'

127

The men stand like shuffling pillars, hands in pockets, with odours of after-shave and cigarettes and the rough sandy smell of tweed jackets, also smiling, and hoping, I am sure, that this scene of mothers and daughters will not turn into a melodrama. But Alex's laugh climbing invisible ladders must reassure them, and the way she twirls off her coat and steps around the table approving of the food. 'Matti, aren't you going to offer us a glass of wine? Pour Mother some wine ...'

'We got beer too,' says Matti, and the men move, relieved.

Alex with wine-glass in hand comes to sit next to me. She holds the glass at my lips and carefully I sip, intent on not dribbling, and the explosive green taste of the wine seems to froth on my tongue. 'Are you really okay, Ma?' she asks.

'Yeh,' I say, 'faai.'

'Do you need anything?'

'Nooo.'

'I've missed you, you know. When you're better, you must visit Damon and me.'

'Yes, you must visit ...' echoes the man, Damon.

I hold my head back and nod slowly.

'Will the doctors assign you a physiotherapist?' she asks, again letting me tongue up drops of wine.

'Madee,' I say, 'Madee.'

'But is she trained?' Alex says, lowering her voice.

'Unuff,' I say.

Soon Damon and David carry my chair to the table and they all sit down to lunch. The young people are hungry and pass the dishes quickly, and Matti spoons small mashed portions into my mouth, mere token portions, knowing so well that I dread making a spectacle of myself. Alex talks about Portland and the radio-station, and her eyes gleam like yellow beryl-stones, her hair so cropped. I think of Nefertiti or Ashtoreth. Her long hands touch, now Damon, now me. She chews in her old hasty fashion and drinks with her slender neck arched, and flirts. Yes, it seems to me she is flirting with us all, but less with me than the others. The flirting is a show she is putting on for me, I surmise, jealousy and pity and anger beginning to block my throat. I motion to Matti to remove her spoon. Why, I ask, does Alex need to display her beauty as if it is a precious stone to be turned this way and that? Why does she, also, so badly need to act as if everything is wonderful, as if we are all happy, as if I cannot perceive that there are no moments of quiet sincerity, no long questioning looks especially for me. Oh yes, we daughters will always expect our mothers to have no concerns except those that touch us nearly, but we mothers in extremity *want* our daughters' undistracted glance.

Now David is teasing Matti because there are no chitlins or collard greens on the table, and Matti pretends indignation. Damon tells a funny story of Alex's undercooked oxtail stew, and Alex is off again with a story of linguine and how difficult it is to throw strands of it against a wall to see if it's done. Her fingers flick and flick, and Matti objects that's no way to treat food, and David up-ends the wine bottle so the last drops drip into Alex's glass, and my innocence drains away in vexation.

I cannot take the cheese-cake into my mouth and my head is heavy with the tears of mortification behind my eyes. When Matti leans forward in anxiety the talk stops. 'Maybe it is too much for her,' says Matti. 'Maybe she had enough …'

When Alex says, 'Let's move her chair back into the sunshine at the window,' some tears, hot heavy and shameful, plop onto my hands. Alex gets quickly to her feet. 'Matti and I will move Mother but … we're out of wine … why don't you guys go buy another bottle from Witruba's Bar? You saw it when we drove in. We need more wine. Okay?' And the men rise hastily, heavy feet moving lightly, their bodies blocking the air from the stairwell as they leave.

129

Alex and Matti lift my chair and carry me to the window. Alex grabs at the footstool and pulls it under her so that she is sitting at my feet. She takes my damp salty hands in hers and says, 'What's wrong? Can you tell me what's wrong?' But how can I explain jealousy, pettishness. I know she is looking up at me, but my vision has not cleared and her face is an oval blur.

The room has become quiet. Matti is slowly, gingerly clearing away the plates and dishes and Alex continues to hold my hands. I turn my head and sigh, and now my eyes dry. Mooney's yard is in broad noonday light with no shadows except the purple circles under the peach and the elm. Alex also sighs and then she slips her arms around my hips and buries her face in my lap. I can feel her warm breath through the velour onto my stomach. I am shocked and then not shocked. I manage to get my hands onto her head of crisp, shorn hair, and so we sit locked. My fingers move over her warm firm scalp, and she breathes and breathes into me, and my chest stops shuddering and I grow calm. I can ask no more than this, no more. Then she looks up at me, red-faced and sly, and we both laugh, soft as idiots.

The men come back with the new wine. After the coffee they'll all leave, Alex and her men to check in at the inn, Matti to take her afternoon break. They will all be back in the evening. Making a gentle burlesque of it, they all help to lift me onto the bed and prop me against the pillows so that I can still see into Mooney's back garden if I want to.

I doze, and when I wake the light has changed and the sun is throwing splashes of brilliance and long magenta shadows. The cat lies stretched on the window-ledge as if its bones have melted. The dogs lounge at Mooney's screen-door. Without reflection, I shift my shoulders and flap my hands against the pane. The cat stirs and yawns like pulled elastic, then lifts itself high onto its legs. A gymnast, it stretches first one long leg backward then the other. Then, silly cat, it leaps. Both dogs sit up. They stand, mouths agape, ears back. The cat is examining something in the grass, patting at it. At a lope, the dogs approach. So the cat reduces herself and thinks of snaking, but Wolfie jumps into its path. Ginger lifts her spine and bares teeth. Wolfie is motionless but Gustave springs, trying to snap at the cat's lower spine. She curls herself round and claws at his nose. Then Wolfie makes his move and catches her small molded head in his mouth. The cat goes limp and I think it is dead already. Moonee, Moonee, I wail. Moooneee ...

But miraculously, she twitches and curvettes and lands on foot-springs at the other side of Wolfie. Like a meteor she bounds onto the sagging wire-mesh fence and swings backwards and forwards lightly, and then flies onto the drainpipe. She stands weightless, twitching, tail whipping and ears back. Then she settles into herself and nonchalantly licks a shoulder before beginning a thorough cleansing operation. But I am panting.

'You still watching them unknackered brutes?' says Matti when she comes in.

'Noo, Katta,' I sigh.

'Well, lets get you to the bathroom.' She bends and lifts my left arm, drawing it over her shoulder, and pulls me to my feet. Then she grips my waist firmly round my back and we stumble forward. 'Maybe someday when you more better we get you a cat. Okay?'

I nod my head but suddenly I know that I don't want a cat of my own. That was never my thought, to own a cat, or any living creature. I will be content, I tell myself, to wait for Alex's visits. Content, for the time being.

GRAVESTONES AND OUTLANDERS

1. You elderly Germans are so gracious. I pass you on the narrow sidewalks of this small town, I stepping off onto the road to make way for you, and you thank me kindly and wish me good morning and good day. You look unquestioning at life's unpredictabilities in your square bodies dressed in good simple clothes, still styled as they were in the forties. You cannot foresee the change. There has been barely a significant change in your village in over forty-four years, in spite of the existence of the American bases.

You serious, jowled gentlemen in well-preserved overcoats raise your hats to me. Really, I do not expect such courtesy. I am a stranger here. A stranger alone, sometimes so alone that I suspect I am slowly disappearing, bodily that is. I am fading. I am becoming merely the suggestion of a woman, as if in a painting by Turner, supposing that Turner had painted women instead of ships at sea, storms, and atmospherics. Soon I could be invisible (except perhaps to Christopher), which state would save you some small trouble.

But you still see me and nod, sometimes smile, and *guten* me, and I am mildly gratified. For you must know that I am a stranger. None of the women in this village of my age look like me. None are as thin and wiry, with collar bones forming shell-like hollows below a tendony neck that has lines circling round, as if some primitive beautician had wound string about it to keep it as upright as a youngster's. None of your wives and mothers wear denim, sneakers, and T-shirts. No one, man or woman, ties her hair in a ponytail, and no one walks at the pace I do. You all stroll or trudge, whereas I stalk or pep along, and when I stop to stare at an old carved door or small dog on a window sill, I piaffer. I am a trotter not an ambler. Only little Christopher, skipping, can keep up with me.

I walk when my work is done, or rather when I can stand the village archives and its smell of dead rat fur and dust-grained documents no longer, and when my cellar apartment transforms itself into a space-capsule, spinning me silently through a dull undappled space, the umbilical cord that would send me tender human voices long ago eroded and trailing behind. I am a great walker and I take pride in striding on and on over cobblestones, recent blacktop, stubble fields, forest paths, and along the vegetal alleyways where street people in smashed hats and gaping shoes recline in doorways.

Guten tag and *danke schon*. But believe me, you don't have to be so polite. Apart from my American dress in a German village, I am hardly worth noticing. I am merely a spare walking woman who has, I suspect, nurtured merely dimly original ideas in her life, who cannot learn your language quickly enough for it to be of use during her stay here, and who worries occasionally and rather pedestrianly (no pun intended) about growing old, too old to trot and walk and dig for information. Some years ago as my younger face began distorting the mirror and bringing forth this older, unfamiliar one, a shape where the skeleton beneath the patterning of skin was asserting itself to suggest its final mould, I could think of nothing less banal than to remain young a little longer. Be beautiful and achieve love. That's all, nothing original. I did not decide that now was the time to read Musil's *A Man Without Qualities*, or watch Fassbinder's *Berlin Alexenderplatz* on video from beginning to end, or to become a Hatha Yogi. No, I thought of no self-improvement plans nor did my mind turn to volunteer work among the pregnant teenagers of my town's inner-city.

Yes, anyone who cares to — but I honestly don't expect you to — can take in the measurements of my body and mind fairly quickly. Unless you want me to explain my research into the Roman foundations of this village. But then, you see, I am only interested in the ancient floor and street plans and these might not be fascinating to you. I would simply prefer to talk about how far and how fast I can walk. I could at this point take you on a guided tour of something like forty square miles of shifting, dappled, perpendicular forest light, and ten miles of heather-scented farm lanes on the outskirts of this town. At least Christopher loves our rambles.

2. No, I don't like attention from strangers. Not that your courteousness is offensive, no, not at all. However, some attention is rude and frightening. Some years ago when I was in Taranto, Italy, exploring the early Aragonese plans for the town, I went walking one afternoon in the silence of the town shuttered for its siesta, and glad at the emptiness of the streets. As I examined the porous limestone carvings on a small but elegant Gothic church, I heard an insect-like buzzing from somewhere behind me. It grew louder. I turned. Two boys were riding a flatulent Lambretta in my direction. Sensible kids, I thought; better to have some fun than to sleep.

They reached me, slowed down, and chug-chugged the machine in pace with my stride. They jabbered at me loudly, but I ignored them. When the older of the boys, a cropped-haired kid of about fifteen, demanded in a high voice some cigarettes, I waved them away, saying firmly, 'I don't speak Italian.' They merely laughed, gunned the scooter and went on ahead. I thought I was rid of them. But they merely made a U-turn some hundred yards ahead and sped back down the street, passing me on the way and yelling something jeeringly. They U-turned behind me and came up again, gabbling in their language which I pretended not to understand. They wanted money.

'Go away,' I said loudly. The boys made finger gestures at me, ones I thought must resemble the 'Spanish fig' gesture made by Bosola in *The Duchess of Malfi*. 'Get going,' I said more loudly, waving them away. They took off, repeated their U-turn tricks, but this time they hopped the scooter onto the sidewalk and brayed it, buzzing, between me and the buildings to my left. I had to step off the sidewalk. When I yelled, 'You stupid louts,' they thought I was hilarious. Again they gunned ahead. I regained the sidewalk and stood with my back to the building, feeling its rough sandy stone against my palms. As the boys returned, circled the machine down the street and brim-brimmed it towards me, I felt in my bag for one of the apples I was carrying with me. I have found it always a good plan to carry fruit with me in foreign cities against unforeseen shop-closing times.

I turned to face the scooter. Even though I had not played baseball for about thirty-five years, I had not been Vassar's best pitcher at the Saturday afternoon friendlies for nothing. I took aim and let the apple fly at the head of the boy sitting behind the driver. His body was leaned clearly to one side and the apple caught him on the shoulder. He jerked and the whole Lambretta wobbled. The driver had to put down his feet hastily to steady it and bring it to a stop. They must surely have had enough now, I told myself, pep-stepping nervously ahead. And they had. But as they passed me for one last time, they called out *Putana, putana*. I knew what that meant. I, a lone ageing woman was being declared a whore to the wide silent street and the smooth blue sky and the muddy-edged Mediterranean. When the Lambretta was out of sight, I about-turned and headed back to the station. Although I told myself I didn't give a Spanish fig for them, I kept glancing around fearfully, my heart skipping at every far-off sound. I don't believe something like this could happen to me in your respectable German town.

3. If things continue to change, as they have been changing over the past few weeks, you will notice me less and less, and not greet me anymore. Your village is filling with new-comers from the East. The hotels and bars are packed out and, I believe, business is booming. The sidewalks down-town are a push and shove of bodies. You slow-walking resi-dents of the quiet neighbourhoods do not look pleased. In shops and buses I overhear grumbling talk of higher taxes and housing problems. The other day in a bar I understood enough German to hear a man say to his companion, 'Ach, if one of them owns a German sheepdog, he claims he is a German.'

It is getting harder and harder for me to trot unob-structed along sidewalks, so I have taken to visiting the *Friedhof*, an extensive and aged cemetery that has an aston-ishingly irregular ground-plan, one that I think resembles (if my memory serves me rightly) the old city of York in Bishop William of Nordhouse's time. In the *Friedhof* I ramble and prowl, for it has unexpected pathways between tree-shaded graves, sometimes leading to a cul-de-sac. And lanes that turn corners onto huge ornate tombs opposite which are stone benches for the tired or the contemplative. The whole area is surrounded by a five-feet high, two-feet thick red stone wall, dating, I think, from the sixteenth century, and is the home not only of the many ancient and old dead but also of towering, abrasive-barked naked-rooted trees, trees which I superstitiously suspect grow only in the *Friedhof* and have no known botanical names.

In sunless unkempt corners the graves are so old that they slope haphazardly sideways or backwards. The trees are large-leaved and unrustling there, and the smell of grass in the moist soil redolent of mushrooms and earthworms.

There I can lose my concern with age, invisibility, and the perpetual change to the maps and the populations of cities and towns. I sit on a stone bench and look at a wildflower covered grave mound and think that it cannot be too bad to lie unthinking, and perhaps softly singing to oneself in that giving earth, with no concrete slab below and above one's melting body as they place so cruelly in American graves.

Some of you must yourselves have taken strolls in the *Friedhof*, and soon the newcomers will discover it and turn it into a picnic spot. For the time being, however, it is a place of relative privacy and cool peace.

4. The cellar apartment in which I live is beneath one of your large square unimaginative private houses built in necessary haste at the end of the war. My apartment takes up only part of the cellar and seems to have been meant for a small, contained and probably agoraphobic person. The ceiling is not too far above my head, and at times I feel as if I am Alice in a doll's house. My bed is a shelf in the middle of a fixture of cupboards and narrower shelves. When I have climbed into it, I can draw a curtain to shut it off and lie, the wooden board two feet above my head, and imagine I am at my own wake.

I don't care much for the family who are renting me this place, but then they do not bother me. Except for the little boy of five, they hardly speak to me. He is a little Coloured boy named Christopher Dickey, and he speaks some English. He wrote his name for me in chalk on the driveway one afternoon. He is the child of the daughter of the house, who has moved away, and a black American soldier who has since been discharged and sent back 'State-side', as they say. So the little boy lives with his grandparents, but only his grandfather cares something for him. His grandmother tries to pretend he is not there, except for certain moments of practicality which she cannot avoid. She wishes, I do believe, to turn Christopher white or invisible. As I have explained, I cannot remain for long periods in my cellar.

5. One evening when a mauve sky lifts itself way above the dense green of the trees, when the *Friedhof* smells of loam and crushed marjoram, I dawdle round the serrated trunk of a barrelly red beech and come to a plot of small graves with Hebrew inscriptions on some and German on others, a circular dead-end I have not examined before. Around the sunken graves, several with headstones overturned either by time or jackboots, the pink old wall circles. I try to unravel the inscriptions, but my back growing tired from the bending, I go to sit on the thin damp grass, resting my shoulders against the wall.

I am soon disturbed by a man in hand-knitted cardigan and a cloth cap, following a mutt on a leash. He nods and greets me, but not in German. I am about to form *Guten Abend* on my tongue, when the dog crouches lewdly on a grave and expels two black turds. I look up at the man in horror, but his eyes are now patiently on the dog. The animal smells its own dirt, circles and ambles, crouches again on another grave and shits once more. I get to my feet, but man and dog have turned. The dog lifts a leg briefly to a tree and then the two are gone, swallowed among the farther trees in the dusky light.

I know he could not be one of you. You do love your dogs and you tend to let them roam freely, and train them to be the most xenophobic of their tribe. Yet you clean their mess from your streets and lawns and would not let them despoil graves.

6. It is growing dark by the time I have cleaned the dogshit from the graves with leaves plucked from the lower branches of the beech. I decide it must be time to go, so begin retracing my steps to the gate. The towering trees, the deepening sky, the irregular white and grey of the stones, as well as the

sunken winding paths give me a feeling of walking into a painting by a young, soulful and depressed Poussin or Courbet. I linger to enjoy my disembodiment. When I get to the large iron gate it is chained and locked.

I try to climb up onto the wall. However, its coarseness has worn over the years to the consistency of plaster of Paris and will give no purchase to my feet. And I am too short to get my arms over it to pull myself up. I shiver as the fearful thought of spending the night in the *Friedhof* takes over my thoughts. I stand transfixed, wanting to cry or at least call out for help.

Then I notice how the branches of a nearby tree touch the top of the wall. My solution is to climb up a branch and edge my way to the wall, get on top of it and jump down to the other side.

I have not climbed a tree in over thirty-five years. But I tell myself I am limber and spry, and the tree with its many clefts and extensive branches looks as if it could be mounted easily, even by someone whose mind keeps circling round the question of an approaching sixth decade and whether that decade is worth waiting for.

With one arm on a higher branch, the other firmly on a lower one, I dig my toe into a crusty jag in the trunk and pull myself up. I stand carefully, steadying my footing and am about to ease myself along so that I can approach the wall, when the idea of climbing to the top of the tree comes with all the force of a sweet seduction. I grab upwards for further branches. The bark is rough on my hands, and the work brings sweat to my forehead which trickles tickling into my ears. But the climb is becoming an exhilaration I had not foreseen. I am in a dim world of scented variegated protective leafy canopies and supportive beams, a world I remember from a far-off time of childhood, or perhaps from my own prehistory in the forests of Ardennes, or from simply reading a fairy-story once.

I am high and safe and unseen and momentarily supremely happy. I get to the highest branch that will support my weight, and then I can thrust my sweating head up and out of the leaves. I see a shadowless pattern of vague headstones, urns, stone angels, and grass below me, and over the wall the streetlights and the headlights of cars and the glow behind windows. Above me the sky is dotted with stars, in places in rows like shirt studs for a boy on his wedding day.

A slight breeze wakes the leaves and the branches sough and sway. I hold on more firmly, hugging the acrid-smelling bark in darkness, not certain whether I can see the branches below me in order to climb down again. But I cannot stay up in a tree till dawn.

I feel downwards with a tentative foot and make contact with a thick branch. Steadying myself, I lower a second leg and then let myself drop slightly, still holding fleetingly onto the branch above my shoulders. I straddle too suddenly and the impact on my bones is so painful that I have to sit a minute, hissing and biting on my back teeth. When the pain has almost throbbed away, I begin to edge myself forward, lifting my buttocks up and down little by little. I will get to the wall and get myself onto it and just slip over to the solid earth on the other side. Or not so solid, given the nature of the place I am in. Surely at any moment the earth could subside and the edge of a coffin brush one's ankle, or one's toe slide into the mouth of a skull belonging to the ancestor of one of you steady burghers.

Holding my breath, I lunge forward and grab for the wall at the same time letting my legs dangle free from the branch. How I manage in the subsequent breath-expelling pain to keep holding onto the wall, I still do not know. I have hit my chest after scraping the insides of my thighs with small branches and twigs. Had I been younger I might be worrying about permanent damage or loss of sexual appeal from unsightly inner-thigh scarring.

141

But within seconds I am over the wall, on all fours in the damp sandy soil, and then up and jogging my way home to the cellar.

7. Along with all the people from the East, a circus has come to town. I am told it is a Polish one for I cannot make out the decorative writing in red on white bunting. 'Do not trouble yourself to go. It will not be any good,' colleagues tell me. You can see the troupe has no money. But I think it will be an amusement for Christopher Dickey and me and I manage to ask his grandmother if I may take him with me to the circus. When she finally understands, she shrugs indifferently.

Christopher is too small to stride across town with me, so I decide we will take the bus. It jolts us to an area of small farms and older houses, all with patches of flower and vegetable gardens. It turns down a sand road and heads for an open field. We can see ahead of us a marquee tent in faded blue and off-white set among trailers and trucks. The same notice in red and white sags from a fence. The bus rocks to a standstill and we, together with some teenage girls, get off the bus.

Holding hands, Christopher and I follow the three girls who have linked arms and are singing chirpily. There are other stragglers heading for the circus tent, though not as many as one might expect. There is an earthy presage of rain in the air and perhaps that is why people are not turning out in their droves. As the bus rumbles off, Christopher and I both turn to watch it go. His little face is serious.

The path we are walking along is soft and sandy, and now the feral smell of animals overpowers the clean smell of coming rain.

I pay the entrance fee at the booth and pull Christopher after me into the dusky blueness of the tent. The benches are fairly empty and we have no trouble finding seats close to the sawdust. We sit close together, waiting. Then there is the sound of intermittent raindrops thumping the canvas and we can see splatters coming through the opening at the apex of the tent. A wide opening.

A group of midget musicians marches in and takes its place at the bandstand at one side of the ring, and more little people dressed as clowns come tumbling, tripping and biffing one another to the centre. Dwarfs or midgets. Dwarfs standing on horseback ride around the sawdust as the band strikes up, and dwarfs in tinsel or black-tie and tails come to bow at the few spectators. A dwarf's circus. I am astounded. Dwarfs mill everywhere, prettily and funnily dressed, and expertly made up, but unfunny and inept. They are not good performers, nor do they seem to be enjoying themselves. I look down at Christopher, ready to smile, but he has a strangely solemn and disapproving look on his face. He moves away from me, gets up, and begins to climb the benches toward the top. It's as if he wants to put as much distance between himself and the dwarfs as he can. 'Christopher, are you okay?' I call. He reaches the topmost bench, turns and sits on it, frowning down at me.

With the music now oompah-ing, the dwarfs run back through the exit, and after a Master of Ceremonies calls out something in a highpitched incomprehensible voice, a tiny animal trainer enters, bows, and explains (I presume) what he is about to do. Four dwarf-clowns bring in circular cut-off piramidal stands and set them at equal distance from one another. The rain has increased somewhat and drops hitting the surface of the stands can be heard like little drumbeats.

The dwarfs make much of their own fear as five tigers are let into the ring to lope with glum boredom round and round to the mild cracking of the trainer's whip. The music increases in volume and clumsy coloratura, and the tigers pick up their pace. There is some clapping. The trainer takes a position at the centre of the ring and, after calling out some command, cracks his whip with force. The tigers run; the people cheer thinly. The trainer cracks his whip again and the tigers jump for their stands. But each jump is an unplanned comic routine. The stands being wet, the tigers' paws cannot maintain a hold and they slide. One after the other they land slightly spread-eagled on the sawdust. The laughter from the small crowd rises, real and bell-like. I myself am gurgling in my throat and then giggling.

The trainer tries again. The music backtracks. The tigers regain a semblance of dignity, and the trainer offers what must be an apology. Again he cracks his whip with force. The tigers jump for the stands, and again they cling momentarily before sliding off and sprawling in shameful but funny loss of control. I find myself hugging my body and rocking as I laugh, my eyes blurring with tears. When I can focus again, the trainer is about to make a further attempt, but Christopher has climbed down the stands and is pulling at my arm angrily. 'I vant to go,' he says. 'Hugly tigers ...'

I let him pull me out of the circus tent and lead me toward where the bus should stop when it comes. 'I hate that,' he says. 'I hate dose hugly small menschens ... ach dorfs ...' he mutters. 'Dey not good. Small and hugly ...'

8. The town is so full of people now that I no longer try to walk along the sidewalks. Even the forest paths no longer engulf me in deep green and shattered sunlight, but explode in the many colours of the newcomers' clothes. As I predicted, the *Friedhof* has become a place of Sunday picnics and lovers' rendezvous, and every time I return to the secluded spot where the gravestones have fallen, there is always someone about. I cannot reclimb a tree and bounce high among the branches because an official walks through the cemetery at closing time, making sure all are out.

9. Although you residents hardly notice me these days, my visibility is returning with the return of those from the East.

They look at me as if I am one of them. They too dress in jeans and sneakers and all manner of oddly outdated and fashionable combinations of clothes handed out by the American Relief Society. They talk to me in bars and question me about life in the United States. Some say they will try to emigrate there.

I don't mind that you no longer *guten* me. In a way it's a relief. I have come to realize that small doses of occasional invisibility are good for the soul, and that too much attention from focused eyes might change the likes of me. In any event I am to return State-side in a few days.

'Ach, you mussn go,' says Christopher, grabbing my hand in one of his hard grubby little ones in a gesture of command not affection. 'You muss vait. Ven my fadder come for me, den you can go.'

'But I don't know when your father is coming.'

'Soon, soon, he is coming soon.'

Unillusioned, Christopher stares up at me with intent eyes, his mouth pursed. Then he returns to pushing a Matchbox car along a road he has drawn on the driveway, murmuring Brmm, Brmm.

10. I stand with my suitcases in front of the house. Christopher and his grandfather stand with me in silence. I can see the grandmother's head outlined behind a lace curtain at the living-room window. We don't talk. I have given Christopher a present of a car and trailer set, but he has not opened it. He holds it under an arm and looks solemnly away from me.

When the taxi arrives, I shake hands with the grandfather and bend to kiss Christopher. He keeps his face stiff. As I straighten myself he says, 'Frau, lady. Vhy you didn vait for my fadder to come?'

'I couldn't. I have to go. But [and here I feel my face suffuse itself with shame], when I get to America, I will find

Mr Dickey and tell him he must hurry to come and get you. Okay?' Christopher studies me solemnly, then he lifts his head up and back to prevent the moisture that has come into his eyes from dripping down. I follow my suitcases into the taxi. As we drive away, I wave but only the grandfather responds: Christopher is looking away.

So, dear burghers, I leave your town with a pain in my throat. But I am satisfied that my work is done, and glad for the human changes I have seen.

I grow reluctant as the taxi draws up at the International Departures terminal. Will I feel an outlander for a time after I arrive home? Will the doses of invisibility I am used to there turn out to be too much after all? I shake myself and force myself to speculate on my chances of finding a Mr Dickey among the eight million residents of South Carolina.

THE MODEL

Stani's face goes red when he sees yet another painting in which our forms have been used as models, as red as Eve's robe, my robe, as my naked body burning through the thin russet cloth rendered so diaphanous by Edvard. When my husband is struggling with emotion, his face is never as ghostly pale as is his image in the foreground of the painting. Those who go pale with passion are people who act: that I came to understand when I lived with Munch's group in Berlin. Stani never acts; that is he never acts effectively nor conclusively. He vibrates, he rustles, he bristles. It has become the source of my remaining lust (for want of something stronger) to be the collaborator in Stani's small storms of anger. And it provides moist satisfactions to me to arrange the aftermath of his grovelling and my own self-observing indulgence. Oh Stani, heavy Stani, with his rounded shoulders borne down by too much cogitation, and his clumsy hands and feet. I have settled for Stanislaw — no one better having offered himself.

When Stani is agitated by ardour of whatever kind, his blood grows redder. Yet that very blood's pumping seems curiously to paralyse him as if that movement alone is all his spirit can endure. When he does find muscle to move again, it is to break a few valueless things perhaps, or beat against walls or doors with a flat hand, or grind his teeth — if there are no nearby walls and doors to punish. The next stage is for him to grab my arm or neck and shake me, much like an unvicious Great Dane reminding a pup of its smaller size. Then he tugs at my hair, but never too painfully. Stani has always had a sharp sense of unpleasant consequences. Very unlike both Auguste and Heini, both of whom could grow bleakly, blackly furious and be capable, one knew, of real damage.

In the old days in Berlin, when my Stanislaw would calm down, he would prepare himself slowly (still shaking a little, lips moving) to analyse the experience he had just undergone and to fit it (he might have to chisel away at its edges, for how single-minded my dearest can be) into his Theory of Human Emotions. Then, when we all lived with Edvard in the old manse, how endlessly he and the others would discuss the human condition (male) while I sat silently against the cushions on the floor, sometimes attending, sometimes not. I could be myself a cushion, or an animal, a large toy, a piece of sculpture, or even a fleshy plant, depending on how I felt, my female condition of no verbal consequence. Sometimes growing bored I would take up my cello and play a little, pianissimo perhaps, and their talk would die down as each sank blank-eyed into his own muddied thoughts.

Now in the gallery, red-cheeked Stani stares at his pallid blue-tinged yellow face in Edvard's painting, a portrait in contemptuous contrast to the gently joyous humid red figures of Adam and Eve in the background, so obviously representative of Munch and me. The eyes on Stani's face have been crudely overdrawn above the paint in charcoal, deadening the expression. His face is, in fact, that of the monster he has always denied resided in himself, a monster he has unconsciously perversely evoked in the past, his hand in the small of my back pushing me toward Auguste or Heini or Oskar. Now Edvard has exposed that monster hugely and publicly. Comically too, I think, for Stani still tends ridiculously to nurse the brute and is doing so now.

Smiling, I touch Stani's arm, but he brushes my hand away. The process has begun. My breathing becomes hot and shallow and then, like the following fire in a gas-oven, in my loins a little lamp is lit. I hear the rough wet sound of Stani's teeth biting themselves. I wait.

Unless he plans to slash the paintings and get himself arrested, which could be out-of-character, there is nothing for Stani to do but begin walking stiff-kneed out of the gallery, one long foot placed carefully in front of the other, his arms lying flatly at his sides, his palms open. His head hangs forward a little with the effort he is making not to break into a gallop of frustration. I follow him leisurely, hoping that if anyone is observing us (I *hope* someone is observing us), I shall seem most tranquil and dignified. If there were a dog present, I know it would run up to sniff at my gown. Not being human, it could smell out my contained excitement and force me to whirl my skirts away and grin at these possible onlookers.

On the gallery steps I take my wifely place next to Stanislaw and again await developments. After a while his shoulders fall, his arms come together, and soon he is clasping his hands in front of him like a priest or a pondering physician — his occupation as psychologist being a combination of both, so he always says. Already his face is cooler, there being merely two red spots under each cheekbone just above his beard.

'Edvard needs, I know,' he murmurs, 'to give line and colour and shape to those moments of emotional stress he has experienced. As he does so, the moments resonate anew, and in repetition resonate away forever, and *he* is released. I know this. I know it is to his good. But what of me?'

Stani unclasps his hands and lifts the one nearest to me to grasp me behind the neck, hard, as if he would push me to my knees right there on the steps. I look down at the grey mottled granite and the grey street. The sky is lightly overcast. Stani's hand is warm on my neck.

'Ach, Gott, why does Edvard keep taunting me?' he asks, suddenly thickly, his face I am sure once again suffused. His tongue sometimes swells when he is angry and I have known him to bite it until blood flecks his lips. 'I thought he had his final satisfaction when he painted *The Dance of Life*, when he

149

allowed himself to repeat your face and figure not once but seven times. *Seven* times, mind you! Oh, how I understood the significance of those seven figures — one for each of us. I understood that the sad black figure was the one he intended for me, while the happy white one was intended for himself, and that each of the other five grey ones were in turn for Auguste and Heini and Oskar and Bernie and Marcus. I understood Edvard's intention of rubbing my nose in the rottenness of what you were, what he had made of you, since *I* was the one who had chosen to marry you. Was that not enough, *enough?*'

'Darling, don't be so crass,' I whisper. 'Edvard is not devoting his life in art to sending you messages.'

'Shut your sluttish mouth!' he grunts, his hand tightening on my neck. I let my head drop until it is almost on my chest. Now he will worry that one of the few passers-by, or someone coming out of the gallery, will notice us. Squeezing once more, he removes his hand.

'Stand up straight, Dagny,' he orders me. I merely let my head sink lower. I stand like a slave, smiling inwardly, examining the tender blue and mustardy lines in the granite of the steps. The clouds skudding coldly overhead send racing shadows across the street.

'Stand up,' he hisses.

'You will apologize?' I ask.

'I will apologize,' he grounds out after a moment's pause. Then he releases a deep shuddering breath. I lift my head somewhat. 'Let us go home,' he says and starts loping down the steps two at a time in a diagonal direction. I hesitate, considering whether or not I should force him to return up the steps to escort me down. But when he motions to an oncoming hackney, I follow Stani quickly, relieved at the thought of being able to sit resting in the clopping silence all the way home. Stani never talks in cabs for fear of being overheard by the cabby.

I relax back and close my eyes. Again I am forced to remember Edvard — each new painting brings the memories back — and those three months of luxurious self-regarding pleasure in which I lived with him, an exalted state that blew its fresh wind into the faces of the other six and made them cold with envy.

It started that day in 1893 when, on leaving the conservatory with Gitta and Annesu, we noticed the artist sitting on the railing and apparently sketching us. He called to us in a jolly fashion, asking whether any of us wanted modelling work. We laughed, calling back *not at all, thank you, Maestro*. Every day that week he was there, calling to us. On the Saturday, as I left the building alone at lunch time, he came up to me and bowing introduced himself. The famous Norwegian. I was astonished. Together we went to Berthe's for Champagne, he carrying my cello case.

He was thin and nervous, smoked too much, chewed at his lips, and was incessantly picking at the shreds of tobacco on his tongue. His eyes were narrow but very bright and really *saw*. He saw me all the time, every line and contour of my necessary body, every undulation in light and shade. I began to see myself for the first time, the way my neck rose birdlike from my narrow shoulders, the light exploding on my hair, the curve of my spine creating the soft marbling of my hips, the cuppable (culpable?) curve of my breasts, and the way my sex disappeared tightly between my thighs. I saw my own smile and the pressure of my cheekbones and thereafter could not stop sunning myself for Edvard, nor resist his presence. He sketched me a thousand times over, and I was terribly happy to be seen correctly and exactly for the first time. To have my body understood. To have my flesh honoured and worshipped perpetually in reproduction. For three months I loved myself as I had never before nor ever shall again love myself. It was not Edvard's love of me (he never did love me as a man) but my own self-love that touched the others eventually with its heat and stirred them. Then each of them — Auguste, Heini, Oskar, Bernie, Marcus, and Stani — thought himself in love with me.

But they were like sufferers of the influenza, alternately cold with envy for an Edvard they could not fathom and hot with the contagion of my self-delight.

Then suddenly Edvard had had enough to feed his imagination. He no longer needed to look at me. For a while I could not comprehend what was happening. Several times a day I would present myself to him like an odalisque or dog, throw myself before him, strike a pose. But his mind would be elsewhere, his eyes opaque as he played with form and assessed brush-strokes. Then began for me a time of aimlessness, of staring in mirrors and weeping.

Like an Eve exiled from Eden and innocence, I had to turn to the earthlings who offered themselves: first Auguste, then Heini, then Marcus, then Oskar, then Bernie. The one then the other, not always in that order. The pleasure in it for me was observing the pique or annoyance of those whose turn it was not. And whether the love-making was boisterous or perverse or flabby, each night I cried. I cried because it seemed Edvard noticed nothing of my loss, my disappointment, or my frantic attempts at diversion. I stopped going to the conservatory. I stopped practising. But no matter.

Had I known that Edvard caught and recorded each fleeting expression, each coupling, each quarrel, I might have become reconciled to my diminished status. But, as I say, no matter now.

When Auguste and Heini nearly came to blows one night over who should have my attention (I was in fact feeding fresh Hanepoort grapes to Oskar), Stani took me aside and most ceremoniously proposed that we marry and move away from the turmoil. I accepted. My happiness with Edvard would never return, that I knew. Because I had not yet made love with Stani, because I sensed the titillation he derived from his own envy, and knew the way he moulded his theories to suit himself, I intuited that with him I would find at least passing amusement in a see-sawing sexuality, in a pleasurably painful powerplay of tension, of calculated restraint and artful letting go. Indeed, we have at rare moments created of ourselves a whorled mandala, curling and curled in turn the one round the other — taut and pliant, pliant and taut.

Stani helps me down and pays the driver. We enter our apartment like a tired old couple. We have still to retrieve a momentum lost in the lolling jolts of the carriage. Stani opens the living-room door and allows me to pass through ahead of him. Another victory. I go to stand at the window in extended studied profile, in the position Edvard painted me in the Linde Frieze, panel four.

Stani paces the room, the warmth of his blood reeking through the thick serge of his clothes, his shoes creaking rhythmically.

'Just how many times did you make love with Edvard?' he asks, as he has so often in the past, his eyes red-rimmed.

'A thousand times, Dearest, a thousand times,' I lie yet once again, not looking at him.

'Gott, oh Gott,' he groans. 'What a life for a man!' He paces again. 'So, I shall have to suffer a thousand paintings,' he adds illogically, stupidly, unable to comprehend that it was my person not my passion that aroused Edvard's artistry.

'Probably,' I say.

'Admit that even after we were married you continued to see Edvard!'

'Stani, you yourself instructed me most earnestly not to break the friendship.'

'Do you always do as instructed?' he asks, attempting to be sardonic. He strides toward me, his hands outstretched for my throat. I draw myself up and look at him coldly.

'No, I do *not* always do as instructed,' I say steadily. Stani hesitates. His hands become soft in the presence of my steadiness. Instead of touching my neck, he reaches for my cloak, undoes the clasp, and with an elegant gesture removes it and throws it across a chair. My victories will accumulate. 'But,' I say more gently, 'like any young wife, I have let myself be influenced by you and your theories. You know this, why do I need to tell it to you again?'

'But ... but could you not simply have obeyed your heart in all matters?' he begs. At this moment he *thinks* that what he most dearly wants is for me to say that I have loved only him and have only ever wanted to be with him.

'You said one's heart should be governed by one's intellect.'

'I spoke of men ...'

'My poor intellect, young and unformed, could not help but be instructed by yours,' I say. Stani looks closely into my face. He swallows heavily, his throat bobbing. I begin to unpin my hair, knowing that when released its springy wildness gives me the look of a solemn child, one seemingly about to approach puberty with awe and humour. Stani's face regains its normal colour and his eyes open a little in what I believe is admiration. I smile slightly. Then he flushes again, not yet ready to abandon the charade. He resumes his pacing.

'If only I knew that you loved Edvard and Edvard only at that time, and could not help acting on that one strong emotion, you, a mere woman, a child in fact, I could accept that and not be tormented. But then, all those others ...' His voice grows thin with self-induced agony.

'I did not and do not love Edvard nor any of the others,' I say coolly. I sink into a chair. Soft rain has started to fall against the window panes. The air is heavy with our sparring breath and I feel my limbs grow lethargic. Stani comes to stand over me, his eyes appalled, his red mouth agape.

'Then I simply cannot understand your behaviour,' he says. 'If you did not love then you must have been motivated by simple lust. You, a young girl! Admit you slipped off several times to see Heini and Bernie, even after we were married. Probably even Marcus ...'

'Oh Stani, don't be tedious,' I murmur, yawning openly.

'I don't want to be tedious,' he replies in some haste. 'I merely want to understand.'

'You told me to feel free to do what I pleased,' I remind him. I look intently into his eyes forcing him to recall chapter and verse of his preaching. How he spoke at length of the essential freedom of each individual soul, of the impossibility of one soul possessing another, of the vital importance of the mind being in control of the subconscious forces. Of freedom, freedom, the beauty of freedom freely chosen. I look at him, willing him to remember.

'Yes, yes,' he says, smacking the palms of his hands dully together. 'I know my own convictions. He straightens himself and goes to stand in the middle of the room.

'Dearest,' he says softly, 'in those days when I spoke, I had in mind the exercise of certain mental strengths a *man* could make over his baser emotions, especially if they were destructive ones. It was for Edvard's benefit that I put forward my views so strenuously. For poor nervous Edvard who used to regard life merely as a sum of hideous obstacles he had to strive against. It was for his own happiness ...' Stani's voice goes dry as he pleads for comprehension, not so much mine as Edvard's. 'For his happiness, I wished to show that through the exquisite pressure of the intellect, we could dominate the ugliness within us and be freed to enjoy the world's beauties. For Edvard ...'

'Stani, neither of us has seen Edvard for over a year. Shouldn't we forget about him?' I say, knowing full well that we will not. I undo the buttons at the collar of my gown.

'How can I forget Edvard's tortured, twisted, grotesque

sense of sin?' shouts Stani, stamping one large foot noiselessly. Ach, forget it, forget it, I will him in silence, knowing
that sin was not in the room when I modelled for Edvard.
He looked and worked, hour after hour, his face intense and
yet peaceful. I looked with him and was happy. Noticing
that I have become distracted, Stani tries a different tactic.

'You know that Edvard hates women, don't you? Look
how he projects onto them, poor creatures, his detestation
of his own attraction for them!'

'Edvard paints what he experienced, what he remembers,' I try explaining but Stani interrupts me.

'Then he remembers me as a monster of jealousy! How
utterly unjust!' He drops to his knees at my chair and buries
his face in my lap. His hot breath penetrates the cloth to my
thighs. I run fingers through his sweating hair. He lifts his
head. 'You know it was to get Edvard to finally recognize the
glories of Creation, the joy of nature, and the loveliness of
male and female in unison that I worked so hard with him
on my theories ...'

'I know.'

'How unjust,' he murmurs, dropping his head into my
lap again. Poor Stani. He will now only ever remember his
own face in the foreground of the painting, forgetting the
idyllic roseate figures in the background, Stani knowing
nothing of the delight of the sight doubly exercised. If he
should again harp on the Adam and Eve figures, he will
have forgotten that Adam and Eve regard each other, barely
touching.

'Utterly unjust,' I echo.

The rain is falling sleekly now and Stani's arms circling
my hips are relaxed. His shoulders rise and fall as he inhales
deeply my scent through my clothes.

'Did you enjoy so much the hands of our friends, our six
friends, on your body?' he asks at last, looking slyly up at
me.

'Yes, but no more than I have enjoyed yours and do enjoy them. In fact [I take in breath] not as much as I enjoy yours,' I say.

'Do you love me, Dagny?'

'Yes,' I say.

'Oh my dear,' he whimpers, his fingers paddling. He lifts my gown to my knees and begins to unbutton my boots.

'Wait!' I command.

'What is it?'

'Apologize!' I say, brushing my gown down to my ankles.

'Apologize?'

'Yes, for saying I have a sluttish mouth.'

'Oh, I apologize, Your mouth is beautiful. A child's, an angel's. Darling, I do apologize …'

'And apologize for holding my neck as if I were a serf or a possession.'

'Dearest, I apologize. You are a free soul, and I adore you in your freedom. I adore your freedom!'

I let myself sink back into the chair and allow Stani to lift my dress. He continues to unbutton my boots. He tugs them off and places my two white feet on his thighs, stroking them and gazing bemusedly down at them. He looks up at me and smiles a small smile that grows broader.

'You clever darling,' he says. 'How you understand me.'

Laughing a little he reaches for my stockings. Happy, he will once again relearn my flesh through his fingers, relishing what he feels, his eyes closed in pleasure. I alone will gaze at my white contours, trying to see again what it was Edvard saw, striving to relive my intensest delight in spite of Stani's plain sweat-drenched zest for concupiscence.

AH, PRAGUE!

Stacey sits facing a small paned window that shows snow-covered rooftops, an unbroken line of lacelike bare trees in the distance, and a sky of sparrow-wing grey. To give herself the illusion of sunlight, she has turned on an overhead light, a lamp on each of the bookcases to right and left, and a standing lamp behind her left shoulder. So that her spirits may not be too low, she is prepared for her electricity bills to be high.

Perhaps it is time for me to look more deeply into our behaviour, into both hers and mine so that I can finally understand what happened and then pack the whole business away like a set of working-drawings for a project that has been cancelled. I believe the affair resulted in more suffering for her than it did for me, because since then she has become something of a recluse, or so I hear. All the better. What I have to discuss cannot now offend her or harm her chances with future, perhaps timid, lovers. Though I find it hard to believe that at her age she should still have that wild and exalted approach to love that I glimpsed in her, a manner that could disconcert a man. Also, surely by now she is 'in the change', as we say.

Our first meeting took place several years ago. I have altered little since that time. I do not look as robust as I used to but I am, in fact, in better health than I ever was. I still ride my Bianchi at least twenty kilometres three times a week, and my abdomen is as hard as a washboard. But because I have lost weight over the years, my cheeks are hollow, and my eyes, always protrudent, stand out as if what I see is unvaryingly distasteful. Yet nothing shocks me, not even my own unpredictability. There are moments when,

159

catching an unexpected glimpse of my own face in a mirror, I am surprised at how cadaverous I look. Yet my hands — my pride — are as supple and smooth as ever. You see, I am an architect and, in my way, an artist.

Stacey had good facial bones and her skin was smooth, but now it must be folded in grooves from nose to chin, and her always large-knuckled hands leathery and brown-blotched. Her over-used eyes behind large glasses are surely retracted into the softening bags of ageing skin. It is possible that her hair is attractively streaked with silver and that she has remained slender, but surely she no longer strides. No, I cannot believe that she still strides with that narrow-hipped, stiff-legged walk she had.

I am still not a South African citizen though I have lived in Pretoria for twenty years. I am from Eastern Europe, but I am in no mood to talk about my country. I do not wish to parry silly remarks about drunken Dubrovnikis or piss-artist Poles. I don't feel like hearing another joke of this kind: Question — what do you call an abortion in Czechoslovakia. Answer — a cancelled Czech. I am not always a humorist.

It is enough for you to know that I grew up in a city where music, art, theatre and literature were knitted into the essential fabric of the people's lives. Unlike you Americans, we did not have to make expeditions to guzzle culture in small but expensive doses. Riding the tramcars, we dropped in on the orchestra or theatre from work or school: culture was as familiar to us as our daily portion of bratwurst and Pilsner. Stacey was by no means too good for me: no woman can ever be that, and I have not yet married.

At about 8.45 p.m. one Friday night, Paul's new white Jaguar drew up with an impatient scrunching of hastily braked tires in front of his friend Westie's house. Inside, Westie and his wife Hilary waited with Stacey, their guest, for Paul to arrive so that all four of them could go out to dinner. Paul had not yet met Stacey, though over the past couple of years Hilary had often spoken of her cousin to him, always ending some anecdote of Stacey's remarkable doings with the words, 'You two should meet. You are *so* alike. You would simply *love* each other!'

At that moment he did not want to be part of this contrived foursome, this planned scenario in which he and Stacey would act out a mutual admiration for the gloating eyes of Hilary and Westie. He had not wanted to drive the thirty-five miles from Pretoria to Johannesburg to meet this cousin who, with great resourcefulness and energy, had left riot-ridden South Africa and had managed to get herself a job in the United States, and who was now being hosted by members of her family as if she were some sort of celebrity. Besides, he had been drinking wine since he closed his office at 5.30, and he was in that pre-drunken stage of irritable clarity and verbal fluency that always drove him into ugly debates, even with people he liked. And he was annoyingly late.

When he entered the living-room, Westie greeted him in a voice loud with relief. Westie had obviously worried that Paul would not show, that he would let them down as he had often done in the past, and that Westie alone would have to conduct two disappointed women to dinner. Westie held him in high regard, Paul knew. *He* was large, drum-chested and broad-shouldered, whereas Westie was short and slight. He was a creative designer, whereas Westie was a plodder. His voice was deep and melodious, whereas Westie's was the usual thin sing-song South African one. He had made a daring escape from his motherland during an invasion, whereas Westie had only ever set foot out of South Africa to vacation on the island of Mauritius.

In the subdued light of the elegant living-room (designed by Paul), the two women sat looking up at his entrance,

Hilary on the edge of the seat about to rise. Their skin gleamed doll-like, he thought. While Hilary got up smiling, Stacey remained seated, her hands in her lap and her legs casually stretched out in front of her on the white fur-piled carpet. He noticed with the instantaneousness of his usual sharp observation how the narrow beam of light from a slender standing lamp expanded itself on her dark head, highlighted what seemed to him a Malaysian cheekbone, ran across a taut collar-bone, dropped down her upper arm, touched her elbow, then emphasized the slim length of her jean-clad legs and her feet in high-heeled sandals. He noticed all this with a stab of pleasure but told himself she had not even had the good grace to wear a dress for the occasion.

'Well, if it isn't my lover-boy at last,' said Hilary, about to throw her arms around his neck.

'I have to use the bat'room,' he said, disengaging himself from Hilary, nodding at Westie, and running through the living-room to the interior of the house, not waiting to be introduced to Stacey and gratified that three pairs of eyes had to follow him. He expected that Stacey would observe with a little shiver perhaps the extraordinary muscled breadth of his shoulders clear under the thin cashmere sweater he had on, and the tight roundness of his hard buttocks in fine wool trousers. Women always told him that the first thing that attracted them to him were his shoulders, his voice, and then his rear-end. One woman had told him as she hugged him, her arms low, clutching his pelvis to hers, that he had two good hammers to knock a nail in. He had liked that little joke.

The others were ready and waiting for him when he came out of the bathroom and he was not formally introduced to Stacey at all.

In the restaurant the dinner began well enough in the always flattering situation of being able to choose food whimsically from a long list. Stacey's voice was low and pleasant, not strident as he had somehow anticipated. She had to put on glasses to read the menu, making her already serious face positively schoolmarmish. At that moment Paul decided that, in spite of her rakish way of dressing and her amiable manner, he was in no danger of falling for this woman described to him as capable of making (as he once was) rebellious political statements, of acting decisively, of devoting herself to — whatever. He could now relax under Hilary's eager panderous glances. A short while later, however, when he was loud and abrupt with the black waiter for bringing their Bellingham Grand Cru inadequately chilled, Stacey put her hand on his arm and whispered to him (she sat next to him), 'Please don't blame the waiter. It's not his fault.' He could feel each fingertip singly and firmly through the cashmere, and suddenly his earlier irritation returned, growing like air filling a surfacing swimmer's lungs. He *had* to release it, and to his credit he did so in controlled outbursts.

Unfortunately the control caused his rich voice to grow raucous, and thickened his accent until to his own ears he sounded like a *muzhik*. This further increased his annoyance. Relishing an awareness that the tension at the table was becoming as palpable as the garlic in the steam from the fungi and calamari dishes, he took over the conversation and dominated it. He began relating the great frustration he was experiencing trying to design a house for a lesbian couple who kept wanting changes. He referred to the women as butches and bull-dykes. Without looking, he knew that Stacey, inhaling audibly, had put down her knife and fork and had turned to him. When she tried to speak, he held up his hand and gave her no chance to interrupt.

He never once looked her way, but he could see Hilary and Westie glance repeatedly and uneasily at her. He understood with triumph that they were struggling between their high esteem for him and their affection for Stacey. They wanted to come to her protection but, with their timid good manners, did not know how. Hardly eating, but drinking steadily, he found himself in that coiled state where he wanted to attack everything that others respected, all that they considered reasonable, decent, or just. He wanted to belittle the image of this Stacey who, he had been so annoyingly told, was like himself — someone who had packed up and left an intolerable political situation and taken her chances in a strange land. He planned to reduce her to impotence and silence and her opinions to trivialities. He spoke on, letting his incensed mind and now awkward tongue handle every abrasive topic, enjoying the configuration in his mouth of words like Jewboy and Nigger, bitch, cunt, pansy and queer. He ranted about the human trash he had to work with and for.

After making a couple of futile attempts to modify Paul's monologue, Stacey opened her mouth only to eat. Eyes fixed on plate, she ate determinedly. Paul wondered whether she hoped that this form of dutifulness to Hilary and Westie might salvage something of the evening's purpose. At one point Westie also tried to stave the current of Paul's speech, saying with a stiff smile, 'Ach Paul, man, let's not be so serious.' But eventually he and Hilary sank into a seriousness of their own, hardly listening but nodding as they jabbed at the food on their plates. They had obviously given up hoping that Paul would suddenly say with a laugh, 'Oh don't pay attention to me, my friends. I have been in an ill-humour, but now I shall joke with you.'

By the time the plates were cleared away, there was no longer any pretence at their table of enjoyment or even simple pleasing satiation. The waiter too had kept his distance, only coming forward when Westie gestured to him for the check.

They returned to the house for coffee. There was an almost benumbed atmosphere in the living-room, with desultory conversation mostly between Hilary and Westie about horses, dogs, the economy, the riots, and hopes for good spring rain. Squatting, elbows on knees, in a beanbag seat, Paul drank his coffee in a lowering silence. He felt enervated now, and the other three seemed thankful that the failed evening was drawing to an end. But suddenly, perhaps his still-lingering fury revived by caffeine, Paul interrupted the weightless random talk and began a story about a Sudanese student who had come to his home town for some sort of training, a story about how astonished some people had been to see their first black man.

'Everyone wanted to touch him, you understand, to see if his skin was hotter or colder than theirs; if it was smoother or rougher, ha, ha. They stared at him wherever he went. They would laugh at him to make him laugh so that they could see his teeth, so big and white. Then the stupid black bastard went and slept with one of our girls. So one night some of the young men grabbed him, ran a rope around his neck and hanged him from a lamppost.' Staring unblinkingly at Stacey, Paul said as he put his coffee cup down, '*They* knew how to handle coloured people who give trouble.'

He had been about to leave before he began the story, but in the short silence that followed, it was Stacey who rose and left the room before he could hoist himself out of the beanbag. She strode out to the passage, and it was then that he noticed her narrow hips and the way she swung her legs with a kind of loose energy. He sank back into his seat, thinking she had gone to the bathroom and wondering how she would try to convey her displeasure at his story on her return. All three waited, but she did not come back. The mood in the room was dull with wordless destruction, but Paul could not bring himself to go without some victory that seemed to be eluding him. Eventually he had to go without it. Hilary was no longer suppressing yawns and Westie made no effort to talk.

Paul drove the thirty-five miles home in a state of trembling spasmodic upset, trying to swallow the bitter beginnings of a hangover plus conflicting surges of self-hatred and self-pity which were the inevitable components of an absurd conviction that flowed through him at the most inconvenient times that all women everywhere should love him.

Why do some men retain that conviction even into rickety and skeletal old age, Stacey wonders as she stares at the early dusk. In her youth, in her prime, in her middle-age, she has known men — ugly, pot-bellied, misshapen, balding, fat-cheeked, stupid men — all of whom would present their penises as if they were gifts, and their mumblings as if they were words of perception and wisdom. Their effrontery was not laughable.

But Paul was not misshapen. He was superbly built, energetic, stylish, artistic; a Bohemian with a voice and an accent that could raise goosebumps on a girl's arms, and an aura of lived history that could make a mature woman lose interest in the normal run of professional or businessmen. For whatever reason: national origin, aura of history, breadth of shoulders, depth of voice, fierceness of beard, hardness of buttocks, stamina of penis, Paul found that wherever he went women attended to him, gave in to him, fell in love with him and let his fickleness hurt them. He, of course, *had* to be fickle: there were simply too many available women.

In the bathroom adjoining her room in Hilary's house, Stacey put her middle finger down her throat and forced herself to throw up her dinner of salad, fungi, calamari, zabagleoni, and wine, for it churned undigested just beneath her sternum. Then she cried until her eyes began gluing themselves shut and her lungs seemed smoke-filled. She told herself that being back in South Africa after such a long sojourn was too much for her. She was out of place and too easily upset. She should have developed an imperviousness to people like Paul and, by now, a dissipation of the shame and fear that the existence of her go-for-white coloured grandmother used to bring her. Deeply regretting her decision to visit her country, Stacey splashed cold water repeatedly onto her face. She wanted to be away, away. Away from ... what? An illogical but real sense of personal menace; the defiant exhibitionism of certain people here; the verbal orgies of mockery and hatred that some political discussions could degenerate into; the steady machine-like awfulness of a man like Paul. She wiped her face with a towel and got into bed, wondering tiredly why she felt wounded as a woman.

Paul spent the next few days in a surly reticence that made the workers in his thriving little business edgy. He had to acknowledge now that there was one woman in the world who, without knowing him as he truly could be — kindly, cultivated, and very good company — had quietly and thoroughly rejected him, a woman who felt contempt for him, who had not even bothered to bid him good-night.

Not all his affairs with women had ended amicably, and he knew there were some who had no desire ever to see him again. That was acceptable. At least if put to question those women would admit that he was a good lover, could be enormously affectionate if in the right mood, and was unusually generous with his money. What he was finding he could not condone was that Stacey should never have the chance of knowing his other selves and growing fond of some of them. He was surprised to discover that he could not bear the thought of remaining one-dimensional to her. Now he *wanted* to retain the admiration for him Hilary must have instilled in Stacey.

Then, too, he could not get the image of her attentive bespectacled green eyes out of his mind, nor the expressive way she moved her rather ungainly hands when she spoke, nor the sense he had of her strength. Hilary had thought that he and Stacey were alike, but perhaps Hilary had been wrong — in a way that disturbed him. Hilary regarded them both as strong people, people who went after the morally acceptable lives they wanted, in spite of enormous difficulties. He suspected that, in truth, only Stacey was strong and that he was a coward, though what kind of coward he could not quite explain to himself.

On the fifth day Paul gave in and phoned Westie's house and a woman answered. It was Stacey.

'Stacey, I have to make you an apology,' he said in a quiet voice that he seldom used, knowing that it could sound like a soothing low-tide sea over sand in a cave.

'Why should you apologize to me?' she asked, her tone rising in recollected anger.

'I behaved myself very badly the other night. I am very sorry. It is hard for me to explain ... I was only a child, you know, when the Sudanese came. I do not approve of what those people did. I should not have said what I said ...'

'You don't have to explain anything.'

He could hear her voice grow breathy and at that his confidence slowly began reasserting itself. He allowed his English to grow formal, to disintegrate slightly, knowing that this seeming evidence of his helplessness often moved women to sympathy.

'I have a great many enormous vorries here at the office, and in truth, if I say it for myself, that other night I vas drinking too much for a gentleman and, I cannot explicate to you vhy, but I get these moods, depressive, no? Irritated, maybe. And I like sometimes hurting people. I hurt your feeling the other night. I insult your intelligence, and I am exceedingly sorry. Dear lady ...'

'Please don't mention it.'

'No, no, you must allow me to apologize and then you must please accept my invitation to a dinner. Please, you will allow me. You will do me the honour?'

Stacey, woman-of-the-world, began babbling, 'Look really I have only a few days left before I return and I want to spend more time with my sister Marcie and I don't think I'll have time for dinner and really I accept your apology but there's no need ...' Her fast speech was for him the nervous back-stepping of an animal sensing an intruder. His voice lowered as he edged closer.

'Vee shall have a dinner together. Quietly. You and me. Please, you do not refuse me. Dear lady, that would be ungenerous of you.'

'Ungenerous? Oh surely not. You see I ...'

'I come for you at seven. Only you and me. Vee shall go together, and I will have occasion to speak to you in a civilized fashion and explicate to you. Without the audience of other people. Please. Certainly you cannot refuse me.'

I am not a superstitious woman. I do not believe in ghosts or Destiny or astrology or lucky numbers. I have inconsequentially broken several mirrors in my life. But I do believe that others can encase us in their own spell of reverence when they insist on our meeting someone they have openly idolized for years and whom they assure us we will idolize too. We are caught in their bewitchment. We approach that new person with something very like love in the sense that we *want* to worship, and we expect at least to be respected in return. We come to the other expectantly exposed, open-faced, offering ourselves at the same time as we hope to consume part of them in something like a communion rite. Others can make two people fall in love, can talk them into it even before they have set eyes on each other.

That first night I looked at Paul with full-grown regard, but he would not make any sign of acknowledgement. So strangely, he seemed offended by my very presence. I could not work out what was happening. The topics he tossed about like so much manure at the end of a pitchfork were, I sensed, not important to him though they were, of course, important in themselves. Yet the apparent bad smell of his own creations made him angrier still. What troubled and did finally insult me was the slowly clarifying awareness that he did not in fact feel *anything* in particular about the subjects he was mishandling. We three were being forced to attend to, be polite to, almost make obeisance to a jumble of lies. And we were forced into a murmuring intimidation by the very pressure with which he was lying. One of us should have had the courage to say, 'Oh Paul, come off it! You're talking a load of shit!' But we all knew that if someone had, he would have smashed his fist onto the table and stalked out of the restaurant leaving us the losers. Of what? you may well ask. Of the presence of some yahoo? No, of the presence of someone we were convinced was heroic, artistic, and in perpetual pain over his native land. Sentimental? Maybe. Things are never simple. Even while I was infuriated by the man, was being made so tense that my stomach wanted to refuse the food I was stuffing into it, I could sense in him sincere griefs and disappointments. They clung to him, as they do to all exiles, like the smoke of burning leaves, acrid on clothes and hair and forming a taste in the mouth. The exile's new world never fulfils his expectations, and his old world will not worsen in his mind: instead it grows sweeter with distance, and its sweetness makes him more bitter.

The morning after that dinner I had a headache, and I felt a peculiar loss of self-esteem that was like a bruise forming. I was short of breath, and all that day I would find myself sucking in air in large draughts. I borrowed Hilary's car and drove to Marcie's house where I spent the afternoon watching her work in her cool garden, following her from shrub to tree to flowerbed, I and her new dog Sebastian.

'Each time I visit this country it seems to get more painful for me,' I said at one point.

'Oh yes, of course,' she said, but she did not ask me what specifically was paining me this time.

'I don't think I'm ever coming back again after this,' I said, with the sullen dishonesty of a child threatening to kill itself. She only stared up at me from where she was crouching. After a moment she said in her usual terse way, 'You'll be back, Stacey.'

Driving back to Hilary's house I came to understand that part of what was upsetting me was the fact that a man whom my cousin had praised repeatedly in her letters to me and with whom she had gone to the trouble to arrange a dinner party, had seemed to dislike me without even looking at me. No reasonable woman can expect everyone to like her, and I had met occasional strangers that had shown me an immediate dislike. But here was a man who had presented himself as a lout and a bigot, and *he* had gone to lengths to show me he cared nothing for my opinions. What further complicated my response to the evening was the belief (based on my trust of Hilary's judgement) that Paul was indeed a remarkable man and that he and I did have things in common. There was this too — I had expected to be attracted to him and had been, like a mechanical toy, set into physical excitement by him from the first moment. As hurt and as insulted as I felt, if I recalled his large powerful frame, his coarse black hair and springy beard, and the grace with which he used his muscular hands, the saliva would flow wetly into my mouth in an impulse of strong lust, all the more shameful because its object was a bully and a liar.

The days passed busily enough for me. I saw Marcie as much as I could and even visited my mother. My breathing had become again an unconscious process and my scalded self-esteem had grown a protective blister. Then Paul phoned and apologized.

It was a Sunday and in Johannesburg many restaurants close on a Sunday so that the staff and waiters can get a day off. I had to drive around the darkened empty streets with Stacey, looking for a place where we could eat. Normally I do not mind driving with a woman. Had I known Stacey better I would have kept one hand on her knee. As things were between us, we could only make the most strained conversation. She was civil but formal and, of course, a little on her guard. I could not blame her. Once I got to know her better I learned that she was not in any case a chattering woman, and never made mindless small-talk. At that time in the car I could sense the tenseness of her caution and I was relieved when we saw a place that was open.

It was a small bistro with poor lighting (poor food as well) and very few customers. It turned out to be a good choice, however, it was quiet and we could be private. Stacey took off her glasses after reading the menu, and I realized, gazing at her over the lighted candle, that she had slightly upward slanting eyes. Yes, she was a beautiful woman, no doubt. I had been careful to drink nothing after work and on this occasion I let her choose the wine — she liked red — and did not impose my favourite on her. Altogether I drank very little that evening.

She began talking about *my* country. She knew where it was, which most South African women do not. She knew what countries bordered on it, what its position had been during the last war, and what its current problems were. I was astounded at first then filled with an expansive sensation of peace. I could talk freely about my country with a person that understood *something*. I almost forgot I was with a woman, I talked so much. I told her about my childhood and my parents. I told her little stories, like the one of when

I was in high school and in gymnastics class. I wanted to impress a girl so I tried a leap I had not done before and I fell and broke my arm. I told her (with tears in my eyes, I could not prevent them) how I had left my parents' home, pretending to be going to the mountains for a vacation and getting across the border to Austria. How I talked and how well she listened. After a pause I conceded to her that I did not like the government in South Africa so well and I explained to her that I treated my black workers fairly. I apologized for disliking homosexuals, but I pointed out to her that that was how I had been brought up and that I liked things to be according to nature.

Later over coffee we both fell silent. She looked down to stir the cup and I was reminded of her womanliness. I noticed the smooth high line of her cheekbones and the soft full way her bottom lip met the more narrow top one. I touched her hand then held it. She did not look up immediately, but stared at our two hands on the table, her face growing a little anxious, I would say. It was then that I realized how badly I wanted to make love with her. Understand me, I did not then have an erection or any other physical sensation of desire. I wanted her in my head, as it were. I wanted to make love to her for days on end until I could extract from her what it was that made her so different from all those other women. I also — I admit — wanted to see her serious face open and then contort with pleasure, to show in the only true way a woman can her subjection to the man, her need, her helplessness.

When I took her back to Westie's house (*my* house, I had designed and created it), Westie's car was not there and the house was empty.

'Vill you permit me to come wit' you to your room?' I asked very softly, lifting both her hands, opening them, and kissing them alternately on the palms. 'Please, Madame ...' As I bent my head close to her chest over her hands I could

173

feel her breath on my hair. I am sure I could hear her heart beating.

She had only five days of her visit before she had to fly back to America. I spent each evening and night with her. She was not like other women, even in bed. This I should have expected, but did not. She did not close her eyes and retreat into some mental cinema which provided an accompaniment to the stimulation of the man. She kept her eyes open, did not mind if the lights were on, and she looked at me, at my body, all the time. I, a man of considerable experience, felt at times a little unusually shy.

On the day Stacey had to leave, I put a necklace of Russian malachite around her neck, a heavy wrought silver bracelet from Spain round her right wrist, diamond earrings from South Africa in her ears, and a ring with a single pearl from the Seychelles for her little finger. She could not wear all together such an assortment of jewellery and we laughed as I put them on and then took them off for her. Trying to control her emotion, she said plainly that she would not go to the airport. But of course she had to go. Then she suggested that I would be happier living in the United States and that I should join her there. Of course I could not. My business was doing well in Pretoria. I had obligations and investments. It was not possible. Not *possible*.

If you have ever been to the Johannesburg airport you will agree that it is the most stupid and badly designed one in the world. Also, because of security, friends and family cannot see the passengers right to the gates: they have to leave them at the entrance and can only watch through a glass enclosure as they descend an escalator to go through security-checks, immigration and customs. Before I left Stacey at the door, I held her very tightly and said, the words coming out as if not from my mouth, 'You will come back and we will marry, no?' Immediately I wanted to cut out my tongue.

As she was about to get on the escalator, she turned one last time to look at me standing at the glass enclosure. It was then that I saw that look of wild exaltation on her face, a look that made me feel as if *I* was the animal sensing the intruder. *Stay in America!* I wanted to shout after her.

I still sometimes wear the heavy bracelet from Spain. I like it. Delicate jewellery looks ridiculous on my large-knuckled hands but not something as heavy as this.

The words I heard most frequently during those terrible months of my return were 'Why did you come back?' At first I would reply that I had come back to be married, but after a while I had to stop saying that. Indeed, within a few weeks after my return it was obvious that Paul did not want to get married and he also did not want to be tied to me in any capacity except that of loose acquaintanceship, broken by irregular nights of love-making: those occasions always of his choosing. Humiliation like a fungus took hold of my spirits, rotting and weakening them. And I was not helped by the realization that my colleagues at the university where I had obtained a temporary job believed that I had not been able to make it in the States, that I had been fired and forced to return to South Africa. Their manner to me was of half-pitying off-handed reassurance, as if to say, 'Well dearie, you did *try*. You gave it a go but it didn't work. Too bad! You'll have to die with us in the revolution after all!'

As I cleared Customs on that first day of my return, I was so overhappy that I was stiff and clumsy, as sporadically forgetful as if I were slightly drunk. I made a mess of the customs and immigration forms I had to fill out, and I had no dexterity in carrying suitcase, handbag, coat, and duty-free liquor. Like a shopping-bag lady I stumbled to where Paul was waiting. He kissed me briefly and took my suitcase. In silence we walked out into a fine dry spring day and headed for his car. I hardly noticed the silence then — I was too delighted by the clarity of the air, the unmarred blue sky, and with being again with Paul. But in the drive to Hilary's house, he was surprisingly ill-tempered, changing lanes swiftly, swearing at other drivers, driving much too fast. Certainly too fast for *this* occasion. Eventually I asked:

'Why are you upset, Paul?'

'I am not upset. Ach, I have been up most of the night playing poker and drinking with friends,' he said.

I wondered why he had needed to be up the whole night before the day of my arrival, whether this was a sign of his intense excitement (I had not slept on the plane), or on the contrary of his taking changes in his stride. But I was really too distracted by the delicate signs of spring on trees and over gardens and then across the bare veld (remember I had come from a landscape covered in the dregs of snow: black, fraying and running at the edges) to give thought then to Paul's card-playing. I was to spend a couple of nights at Hilary's house until I could move into an apartment. I also had a week's freedom before I started work and I looked forward to spending seven fat days and nights with Paul — in whatever mood he was.

Hilary had gone out of her way to plan a pleasant luncheon. The lawn was mown, the swimming pool impossibly blue, and the garden furniture arranged near a glowing barbeque. Both she and Westie seemed extraordinarily pleased to see me again and to have Paul there too. Westie, to please Paul, had chilled the Bellingham Grand Cru to the exact temperature required, and while he poured for us Hilary got the tiny marinated steaks and long kebabs ready for grilling. She had made several different salads and had even baked a couple of small wholegrain loaves. And Hilary was not fond of domestic work.

'People, I can't stay!' said Paul suddenly, hastily finishing a glass of wine so that some dribbled on his shirt. He brushed at it angrily.

'What?' said Westie.

'Paul, you must be joking …' said Hilary. Paul looked at me, recognizing my shock.

'I have got a lot of work at the office …'

'Paul, for Chrissakes, it's Saturday!' said Westie.

'… but I come back to see you tonight,' he said, bending down and kissing me. His nicotine breath was harsh in my face. 'Ciao,' he flung at Westie and Hilary and loped out of the garden.

'Well I'll be damned …' exclaimed Westie.

We three made a pretence of eating.

'Déjà vu,' said Hilary, 'except that it's not an illusion.'

'You mustn't take notice of what he does,' Westie said to me, himself perplexed. 'You know he's strange: you know that. He always does unexpected things. He's been through so much …'

'He probably does have some crisis at the office,' Hilary conceded, her face crumpled with concern for me.

'Probably,' I said. I could not believe it, though, but did try reassuring myself of his close attachment to me by thinking of all the letters and phone calls we had exchanged over the past months. He had told me he paid more in phone bills during that time than he paid in rent. All the same, that afternoon on the green grass at the side of the pumping gurgling pool, the smell of sizzling meat in the air, I could not avoid examining at the edges of my mind the significance of letters that had sometimes been illegible, and phone calls made by him at what must have been 3 a.m. his time, calls on which his voice came across turgid with drunkenness and misery. That he had been trying to tell me not to come seemed a dreadful possibility during that muted meal in an otherwise perfect white South African suburban setting. I was relieved when an hour or so later Hilary insisted that I should rest so that I could start recovering from jet-lag. I drew the curtains and lay in the room, darkened and yet gilded from the fierce sun behind the brown curtains. I tried to talk myself out of the fear that I was about to be imminently deeply wounded. I braced myself that afternoon as from the next room Westie and Hilary's voices came low and anxious in troubled consultation.

Later Paul did come back as promised, bringing with him two gifts, one a beautifully stitched suede jacket, and the other a large book of Karel Plicka's photographs titled *Praha ve fotografii*. On the inside cover he had written, 'All the best, Paul.' I tried not to cry as we made love. Afterwards, as he dressed, saying he could not stay the night, I could not cry although my eyes felt like hot stones and the tendons of my neck ached.

During the days when I was settling into my apartment, he telephoned regularly, and he did come to see me. But he was always in a hurry, always complaining about the pressures of his job. Sometimes he would break dates, or turn up very late — too late for us to go out. At other times he would arrive drunk and maudlin, and spend the evening repeating and repeating how sick his heart was for home and weeping in a way I had never before seen a man weep. Nor have I since. The words of a poet came to mind: Don't give pity to a Czech for you will never be able to stop.

One night, late in October, I listened to his sobs but with distraction, and found myself comforting him perfunctorily. Two days before a young Indian activist had died while in the custody of the police, ostensibly having thrown himself from a tenth-floor window. *That* was on my mind and my own fear that I had trapped myself in a country that would never be a just and humane place, and that I had thrown away the kind of opportunity that comes only once in a life-time by leaving the United States. Paul had not even heard about the young man's death, nor was he interested.

I must acknowledge, though, that there were days when he would be at my door in great good humour, hugging me as if to break my ribs, ordering me to wear his favourite dress for we were going to the best restaurant in town. He would treat me as if he adored me. Once he said to me across a restaurant table:

'It is so relaxing for me to be with you. You are not like other people. You listen carefully when I talk. You are intelligent. Other women always look around to see who is in the room, who is looking at them, never attending or understanding!'

'Thank you,' I said, not smiling, interpreting the compliment as he intended it, as his confession that he was seeing other women! Ah, he could be subtle!

One night, too, after making love to me with an almost frantic passion, he said, 'Oh, you are beautiful ... I love you ... but I hate you ...' By then I did not want to wrestle with what he meant so asked no questions.

What was very hard for me to bear during those months was not so much his faithlessness and unreliability, even as a friend, but rather my own inability to break cleanly from him. My own love, if love is what it was, had grown Rasputin-like and, in spite of what should have been mortal wounds, stayed alive though I was myself inert. Shamelessly, my lust for him had no remission. No matter how disgusted I would feel on an occasion when he was harshly drunk and roughly slurring, I could not maintain a decision never to see him again. I could not resist him if he touched me. I do believe there was more than lust on my part, though. I had an expansive affection for his large head and rough beard. I was enthralled, the way a young mother is with a newborn, with the shape of his hands and feet, the slope of his shoulders. My sweetest memories are of being with him, driving some place, and he being in a good mood. He would start singing Moravian folksongs and I would be moved and saddened, and yet would feel peculiarly happy. In a way, too, I grew to understand his wilful brand of loneliness. He chose to be lonely, and I don't think he had enough self-awareness to recognize why he made the choices that he made. But he was not a happy man and for that I had to pity him. I had taken pity on a Czech ...

Then one night Paul knocked at my door, waking me. It was very late, but of course I let him in. He undressed immediately and climbed into the bed with me. His love-making, after a moment or two of uncoordinated caresses, became a physical attack. He took hold of my hair and tugged my head back. His teeth bit my bottom lip, and he thrust himself into me as if his penis were his last weapon. As he bashed and bashed himself into me, unable to reach his fullest pleasure, he grunted, 'You bitch, you bitch!' his voice drowning out my gasps of pain.

That night my physically hurt body shuddered and trembled until the confusion and paralysis of my mind were shaken out. Then I cried, fully and noisily as a child. Now at last I could see clearly: perhaps because I saw clearly, I could cry. The next day I told my boss that I would not be staying for the term. Although I had given up my job in America, I still had a valid visa, one that allowed me to obtain work. I bought an airline ticket, had a serious talk with Westie and Hilary, and some three weeks later was back at Kennedy, standing in a long line to go through Immigration. I felt deeply patient and tired. I was content to feel tired, to feel tiredly rescued.

Now I teach in a small college on a hill overlooking Lake Huron. My students are the descendants of Finnish and Swedish immigrants. We all live in isolation, in a woody landscape that is snowbound for some eight months of the year, in a community that retains a sombre hardihood against the cold and the dark, and in which strange bitter suicides and killings take place at irregular intervals. But I string up coloured lights before Thanksgiving and leave them lit along my eaves until April. I am often quietly happy, especially when parcels of books and records arrive in the mail, dropped off by the twin-engine Cessna that lands on our airstrip once a week. I have friends, men and women, and there is a man who stays overnight sometimes. During the long winter nights I do have a recurring dream of driving across a wide undulating veld, the grass blowing golden. It is dry and mottled in places by black patches of burn — the usual small winter fires. There is an unending, utterly unvaried blue sky. With the smell of grass and sand in my nostrils, the taste of grass-ash in my mouth, and the winter sun warm on my head, I wake up panting with longing. Paul is singing a Slovak love-song.

Tomorrow I turn fifty years. They have written me that my mother has died. Now there is no one for me in Prague. Ah, Prague.

The blacks are rioting again in this Godforsaken country.

I have a new girlfriend. She is only twenty-two, still at university, and a wonderful gymnast, such as I was at her age. She is a child, however, and I do not respect her opinions. Tonight she has homework to do, so I am alone. The Bellingham Grand Cru tastes sour, but as usual I am drinking too much of it.

When I was in Geneva, after leaving Austria, after leaving Prague, I had a choice to go to Australia or America or South Africa. America? I remember thinking, bah, what a country of nonsense that must be — Vietnam War, black civil rights, women on the march, and all that crime. No one to put a firm hand on things. I came to South Africa and I am not sorry. I have a good living.

If they come rioting near my house, I will shoot at the bastards.

And who knows what is freedom. If Stacey is more free than I am, I wish her luck. If she does not miss me, I am pleased. I do not know where else or how else I can be, and in a way the story is over.

181